I0621447

STOLEN FATE

A Mythean Arcana Novella

Linsey Hall

DEDICATION

To Elaine and John Thomas, for being so supportive and
sharing with me a bit of your artistic ability.

ACKNOWLEDGEMENTS

Thank you to everyone who helped create this story. Your help has improved the story immensely. Thank you, Ben, for the countless hours you put toward getting this book into publishable shape. Thank you, Catherine Bowler, for your eagle eyes in proofreading.

Thank you, Emily Keane, as always, for your help and support. To Doug Inglis, thank you for brainstorming help and amazing ideas. Thank you to Valerie Hayward, Barbara Ankrum, Simone Seguin, and Jena O'Connor for various forms of editing. The story is much better because of your expertise.

Dear Reader,
I hope you enjoy this story as much as I enjoyed writing it.
Happy reading,
Linsey Hall

CHAPTER ONE

Blisteringly hot hellwinds scraped across Ian MacKenzie's flesh as he hoisted the great stone block into place. His muscles burned as he shoved it into position, and the manacle affixed to his ankle cut into his flesh. Why they made them wear these things, he had no idea. It wasn't like the prisoners were going to flee.

A desert wasteland stretched out as far as he could see, burning sands surrounding the cathedral they built in hell. Certain death awaited them in the desert, which was saying something for an immortal. It was nearly impossible to destroy the body of one of their kind, but the hellish afterworld called Moloch could do it.

"It's wrong." The voice of the overseer boomed from behind him.

Rage burned in Ian's chest, searing his ribs and lungs like hell's fire. *It was always wrong.* The great stone walls of the partially constructed cathedral soared above him. He called it a cathedral, but he had no idea what it truly was. No one ever told the prisoners what they were building. But the labyrinthine structure was never up to the standards of the designers.

"Do it again."

Ian ground his teeth and picked up the sledgehammer that he used so often it was driving him mad. He swung it at the stone wall, pain singing up his arms when the hammer connected with the stone. Something in his soul tore away as he destroyed the wall over which he'd toiled.

He kept up the motion until the voice of an overseer echoed across the red sands.

"Enough!"

Thank gods. His muscles burned, his skin stung from the hellwinds, and his mind felt near-fractured from the constant repetitive toil of build, destroy, build, destroy. One of the three overseers unlocked the chain at his ankle and Ian followed the other prisoners, a dozen of them in total, to the departure area. It was nothing more than a patch of sand guarded by two of the overseers. He joined the rest of the men in line to be transported back to the prison.

When he reached the front of the line, the third overseer appeared out of the air. Ian didn't bother to look at him as the cloaked man gripped his upper arm and aetherwalked him back to the Immortal University's Prison for Magical Deviants in Edinburgh, Scotland.

Ian cursed the aether, that ephemeral substance that connected earth and the afterworlds, as the heavens and hells of all the true religions were called. Select Mytheans— supernatural individuals who lived secretly alongside humans—were able to travel through it. It allowed the overseers to transport him from the hellish prison to the even more hellish afterworld every day for his work shift.

As soon as he was shoved into his small stone cell back at the prison, his skin began to feel tight. The walls closed in on him immediately, as they always did.

Ever since he'd been thrown in here, life had alternated between the painful misery of toiling at the cathedral on Moloch and the claustrophobic hell of his cell. His mind felt like it was about to crack from the strain.

He scrubbed a hand over his face and grimaced at the grit. He felt like little more than an animal as he walked to the shower in the corner. It was no more than a hose over a drain, but it washed away the dirt carried by the hellwind.

He pulled on another pair of the ubiquitous black pants and sweater that he'd been wearing every day for nearly a century and settled onto his bunk to count the stones that made up the walls. And dream about the past.

Ian jerked when the door to his prison cell swung open. That was off-schedule. Nothing was ever off-schedule at the prison.

He surged to his feet and watched the burly prison warden escort a small figure into the cell.

His breath caught in his throat and his spine stiffened.

It was a *woman.*

Every muscle in his body tightened. He hadn't seen a woman in nearly a hundred years. And this one was pretty.

Her shining brown hair was pulled back from her face, and she wore *trousers.* And a tight leather jacket. *Gods.* Times had changed.

He dragged a hand over his mouth as his gaze traced from thighs to hips to breasts, devouring. The fabric clung to curves and muscles, so different from the gowns of the women he'd seen when he'd last been a free man.

An attractive woman used to make him stand up straighter, adjust his cravat. The vanity that he'd possessed before his interminable prison sentence didn't stir. But the rest of him did. Made him want to kick the guard out the door and get to know her better.

"To what do I owe the pleasure?" His eyes raced over her face when she stopped a few feet in front of him. Strong features and a determined gaze. She had an expression that looked like she'd roll over anyone who got in her way.

"Can we have some privacy?" she asked the warden.

The idiot in his pants twitched at that. He shifted so that it wasn't evident.

"I'll be just outside the door." The guard leveled a warning glance at Ian. He left the door cracked behind him.

Her gaze met his. Steely eyes—both in color and hardness—searched his own.

It made him wonder what she saw. Once, he knew she would have seen someone stylish, wealthy, good with words. A man with a silver tongue who knew how to get what he wanted.

He didn't see that man in the mirror anymore, and he had the feeling that, on the day he finally got out of this damned place, that man wouldn't return.

No, she'd see a harder man, half animal by now. Shaped by his time in prison like a canyon carved out by a river. The qualities of that man, well, even he wasn't familiar with them.

"I'm Fiona Blackwood." Her accent was local like his, and he assumed she'd grown up in Edinburgh, too. Though the prison contained inmates and staff from all over the globe, her Scottish burr was distinct. She didn't reach out to shake his hand.

It reminded him of what he'd become and that there was no reason to engage in the social pleasantries that were once second nature. "Ian MacKenzie."

"You're in here for blowing up the west wing of the Scottish Museum of Antiquities," she said.

He shrugged. "Aye."

Her jaw clenched. Apparently she didn't like his blasé attitude about the catastrophic damage he and his partner Logan had caused while trying to rob the museum a hundred years ago. It should have been an ordinary job, but their magic had gotten out of hand.

"That's it? You doona feel terrible that you destroyed ten thousand years of history? Bronze age swords and jewelry? Viking hoards and medieval art?" she demanded.

"Aye, of course. I wanted to sell them. Blowing them up and getting locked in here wasn't part of the plan."

She huffed a disgusted sigh. Didn't like that, did she?

"What do you know about the enchantments at the museum?" she asked.

Everything. But he didn't give anyone anything. The habit had started early in his life, back when he hadn't had anything to give. When he finally had, he couldn't see the point. It was no way to survive. "And why would I give you that information?"

"I could get you out of here, if you're interested."

The muscles in his shoulders tightened. He tried to force them to relax, to hide the thrill her words elicited. He had so damn little power in this place already, he hated to give away any more by showing how much he wanted what she offered.

But it was foolish, wasn't it? Of course he wanted out of this endless hell.

"Could you, now?" He tried to stifle the raw desire in his voice.

"Aye. If you help me get past the enchantments. You're the only Mythean who can get through the museum, from what I hear."

"And how did you hear that?" Only one person knew about that, and Ian had nearly given up hope that Logan would get him out of here.

"A thief that I've been looking for tipped me off that there's something I want verra badly inside that museum." Her voice shook, betraying the depth of her desire for whatever the museum kept from her. "And he said that you know how to get through the enchantments that protect the vault."

Logan. Ian focused, straining not to reveal the thrill that ran through him. Was this the day Logan would finally get him out? Whatever the plan, he was in if it meant an escape. "Aye. I can get through the enchantments."

"You're sure?" She sounded doubtful.

"Of course. I put them there, did I no'?"

"Why the hell would you enchant a mortal museum? What the hell were you thinking?" Her voice gave away how incredibly stupid she thought he was. Mytheans were forbidden from revealing their existence to mortals. As long as a Mythean looked human, he could walk among mortals, interact with them—hell, even sleep with them. As long as he never let the mortals know that the things that went bump in the night were actually real.

Break that rule, and the Immortal University would come down on your head and toss you into this hell for as long as they saw fit. They took their job of protecting the secrecy of their kind seriously. Though many Mytheans possessed powers that mortals could only dream of, they were vastly outnumbered. If the witch hunts had taught Mytheans anything, it was that it was best not to spook the mortals.

He had most definitely spooked the mortals.

"What did you hope to gain by enchanting the museum exhibits?" she prodded.

Ian snapped out of the memory of arcs of magic shooting across Edinburgh's night sky, billowing plumes of purple smoke blocking out the moon, and mortals running screaming through the streets. "Why do you care?"

"If I'm going to get you out of this hellhole, I want to know what landed you here in the first place. The only thing on record is that you blew up the museum and alerted dozens of mortals to the existence of magic. It was a shit show. The university had to wipe memories and put down the mortals who were too stubborn to forget what they saw. But you've never said why you blew it up in the first place, and I'm guessing it has to do with the enchantments that Logan told me about."

No, he'd never said why the museum had blown up. The university hadn't cared. All they'd cared about was the explosion and who was responsible. They'd thrown him in here and hadn't looked back.

If it would help him get out of here, he'd tell her anything she wanted to know. "I made a living stealing artifacts. Mortal artifacts sell quite well on the black market. My preferred museum was the Scottish Museum of Antiquities. Eventually, other thieves decided it was prime hunting ground as well. I enchanted the museum exhibits to stop my competitors before they got to the best bits stored in the vault. The enchantments only activate in the presence of Mytheans. The museum blew up that night because other thieves tried to use counter-magic. Something went wrong."

"So Logan was your partner?"

"Nay." It was a lie, but no way in hell was he ratting out his friend. The night that the museum had blown up, Logan had managed to escape. Ian, knocked unconscious in the blast and buried under an enormous pile of rubble, had not. "What's there that you want so bad?"

"The Book of Worlds. Mortals have it in the museum."

"What's that?"

Her jaw slackened. "How could you no' know about it?"

"Never had any reason to know about it." He folded his arms over his chest. He hadn't had the same education as most Mytheans growing up. It had bothered him once, but no longer. Prison had hardened that type of concern right out of him.

"Well, it's the single most important book in the world. To Mytheans and to mortals, though they doona even know it exists. It's a record of all the true religions."

"Interesting, but what's the big deal? Mortals would no' believe it anyway. They're too stubborn."

Though Mytheans were the creatures of myth made real by mortal belief, mortals had no idea. They still fought over the one true god or the one true afterlife. They'd never accept that mortal belief had birthed everything from the gods and mythic creatures like witches and demons to the afterworlds where mortals went after death. It'd be terrifying to realize, particularly since Mytheans now existed independent of mortal belief.

"In the back of the book is a covenant signed by all the gods—Greek, Norse, Hindu, Christian, *all* of them—promising no' to interfere on earth to gain more followers or more power. If it's destroyed..." She gave him a loaded look.

"The gods would no longer be bound by their promise," he said.

"Exactly. They could come to earth and wage divine war. No' all pantheons are power hungry, but it's in the nature of gods to seek worshippers. Many of the ancient gods' followers are dead, and they miss the adulation. They'll seek new ones, here on earth. And of course the mortals will fight amongst themselves to prove which god is best."

He whistled low. So not only was the book real, it was important. Damned valuable, too. His fingertips tingled.

"Why is the book in the museum?" It hadn't been there when he'd been a free man or he'd have stolen it.

"I doona know. And Logan will no' tell me unless I get your help in retrieving it. He thinks my only way into the museum is with your help. I can get you out of here for the time it takes to retrieve the book. After that, depending on your behavior, the university will reopen your case and consider an early release."

His fists clenched. "The university does no' change its mind. I'm in here for another two centuries."

"They might. And this is your only chance." Her voice was hard, but desperation crept in at the edges.

She was lying about the university, and she wanted this. Very, very badly. Why, he wasn't sure. But he was her only shot if she wanted to get past the enchantments he'd placed on the museum.

"Well?" she asked, a brow arched. "Are you going to help me?"

He nodded. No question—he'd take any opportunity to get out of here. He'd see what Logan had planned, and if that didn't pan out he could just steal the book for himself and barter his release. Either way, freedom, that elusive dream that was once so far away, was too close now to prolong it with questions. Questions could wait. Everything could wait, until he was on the outside.

"Good." She reached into the bag at her side and pulled out a circular piece of metal. She held it up. "You'll have to wear this."

Fuck. A gods-damned collar.

"It's been spelled so that you canna get more than ten meters from me. You also will no' be able to use your invisibility. That had to be added specially to the collar. But considering your talents, I think it's worth it."

An angry flush crept into his cheeks. Collared like a damned dog. Like a pet. That'd kill any chance he had of escaping. He realized that she was watching him with calm gray eyes, as if she knew how much this pissed him off.

"Will it negate my other powers?" he asked. He had a mixed bag of talents, courtesy of his Historius and Sylph parents. The Historius side allowed him to find ancient, valuable artifacts and work a little magic, while the Sylph side allowed him to become invisible even though he wasn't a full-blooded air spirit.

"Your Historius talents will remain, but it will diminish your strength and speed a bit, so that you canna turn on me." Her face hardened.

"Fine." He jerked his head. Even without his Mythean strength, he was far stronger than a mortal. He was stepping into another prison, but at least this new one didn't have four walls. It would make stealing the book more difficult, but he'd worry about the damned collar when he got out of here.

"Good." She stepped toward him.

The clean scent of her—no perfumes or fragrant lotions—wrapped around him. Soap, her skin. Nothing more. When he'd lain in bed at night, alone, so fucking alone, he'd dreamed of all the things a woman could be. The shape, sound, smell of her—in his mind, it had always been sweet scents, flowers and perfume.

But this woman smelled of none of what he'd wanted for so long. Yet she had ensnared his mind all the same, lighting up long-neglected needs. She stood so close he imagined that he could feel the heat of her radiating against his arm. It made his skin prickle with awareness.

The guard stepped into the room. "Everything all right?"

"Fine." Fiona pinned him with a steely gaze, trying to take control of the situation. To take control of him.

He held out a palm. "I can put it on."

He didn't want her to collar him.

"I have to do it. It's part of the spell, so that it knows I'm the one it canna leave."

He frowned, then jerked his head in assent, and she stepped closer. Effortlessly, she broke the collar in two and raised the halves of dull metal. Every muscle in his body tightened as her arms neared, anticipation and nerves burning through him. The reaction pissed him off.

There'd been a time when he'd been the one in control, able to move a woman with his charm. Make her melt, make her want, make her ache. No longer. Prison had taken his smoothness and turned it into jagged need.

She was so close it made his muscles tense up and his cock harden. Her gaze was riveted to his neck. He could feel the guard watching the strangely intimate moment as she clipped the two halves in place around his neck. Her fingers brushed against him, hot as a burn, and his nerves lit up all the way to his cock, like a live wire connected the halves. He sucked in a breath to get himself under control. The metal, only a centimeter in diameter, rested at the base of his throat, heavy and obnoxiously symbolic.

"Done," she said. "Now me."

His eyes snapped to hers. She handed him a smaller circle of metal. A bracelet.

Too bad. He wouldn't mind collaring her.

He took it and she held out a wrist. "They'll link us. If you exceed the ten meters' distance, your body will freeze up."

"Will yours?" Sounded like a dangerous damned device if they were in a bad way. He'd be trapped.

"Nay. And I'm the only one who can remove your collar."

So she was the one he'd have to convince to remove it. He drew in a deep breath and broke the bracelet in two as he'd seen her do with the collar. Though it had looked like a solid circle of iron, it broke easily in two places. He raised the pieces to her wrist, both desperate to put the thing on as quickly as possible and to stroke the pale skin of her wrist.

He clipped it on her and stepped back, his eyes lingering on the circle of metal that linked her to him.

"Good. We'll go." She turned and headed for the door.

That was it? He was free to walk out? Just follow behind this no-nonsense woman and out into the sunlight?

Fine by him. He followed his savior out the door, his mind buzzing with the possibility of freedom.

Fiona, she'd said. Tough, and a little bit ruthless from the look in her steel-gray eyes. But damned if he didn't like her. Hard not to—she was getting him out of this place.

CHAPTER TWO

Holy shite, it worked.

She'd just busted a prisoner out of jail. And not just any prisoner. A tall, muscular, dangerous-looking one whose eyes felt like they were burning into her back. He was too handsome for her sanity, with black hair and black eyes that saw too much. He looked like a poet but was built like a warrior. A warrior who would help her get that damn book back.

Fiona marched down the stone hallway like she had every right to be there. Which she did. *Sort of.* After Logan had delivered his odd message to her this morning and said that Ian was the only one capable of getting through the museum, she'd gone to Lea, the highest-ranking university official that she knew, to plead her case. Lea was the historian, and one of the top three officials at the university. They were the only three with the unilateral ability to grant prisoners temporary release. Thank gods she was also Fiona's closest friend.

Lea had agreed to provide Fiona with the documents that would release Ian temporarily, on the condition that he wore the collar, which would ensure that he couldn't make a run for it and couldn't use his most dangerous magic. So they should be fine—as long as they made it out of the building and no one asked too many questions. Even though Lea had okayed Ian's release, Fiona's boss, Darrence Wright, sure as hell wouldn't like the fact that she'd taken matters into her own hands. Utilizing prisoners for intel was definitely not in her job description at the moment.

But she *had* to get that book back.

"I'll lead from here," the guard said from behind when they walked through the entrance to the prison, which was in the basement of the building that housed the Praesidium, the university's security division.

The guard walked past her and pushed open the door to the stone staircase. His were the only handprints that could activate the door. And only if they were alive and willing. She and Ian followed him up the stairs, eventually alighting on the first floor of the Praesidium.

"Thanks," she said, then nodded at Ian while trying to keep from appearing too rushed.

The Praesidium, named when Latin was still the language of knowledge, provided security services for the university. Now she and Ian would have to make it through the building without being stopped. No one would recognize Ian, not after nearly one hundred years down below, but the collar around his neck marked him as a prisoner.

But he'd ditch her without it, so it stayed on. She shot him a look that she hoped said *let's move*.

His eyes lit with understanding.

Good, he could read people well.

She walked quickly, nerves making her chest feel tight. He followed her down the stone-paved hallway, his presence huge and looming behind her, and through the beautiful atrium of the entrance hall. Gray clouds hovered over the glass dome in the ceiling, casting a dim light on the wooden floor. They crossed it and pushed out through the great wooden doors into a cold January day.

She heard him inhale deeply from beside her, pleasure plain in the sound. It struck something within her, something that mourned for the years he'd spent locked up, though she barely knew him and definitely disapproved of what he'd done to get himself imprisoned.

"Air taste better when you're free?" she asked.

"Hell of a lot better," he said as he followed her down the grand stone steps. The pleasure was thick in his voice.

He'd be thrown back in prison when this was all over. She felt guilty about it, but it didn't stop her. *Whatever it takes.* The motto had served her in the past and would continue to do so.

She finally had a chance to fix her life. To fix what she'd screwed up so badly. For ten years, her life had revolved around her failure to locate the Book of Worlds, as she'd been prophesied to do. Hell, it still revolved around it and probably always would.

Five different fate gods had prophesied that she'd return it to the safety of the university. And she'd failed to find it. *For ten years.*

That book defined her. It was everything that made her special, everything that made her a failure.

Her skin prickled as they strode across the cobblestone parking lot, around the great oak in the middle, and toward

16

her little hatchback, which she'd parked in the shadowiest part of the lot. It was lime green and stood out like a priest in a brothel. She had no reason to be parked at the prison and didn't want anyone noticing her car.

No sooner had the thought crossed her mind than a car door slammed. She jerked her head to the right and caught sight of Cerus, one of her colleagues in the Department of Magical Devices. Francis climbed out of the dark sedan after him. Her spine stiffened as they glanced at her and their mouths twisted in a sneer.

Her head snapped back toward her car and she picked up her pace, her cheeks burning with shame. She prayed they didn't catch sight of Ian's collar.

"Friends of yours?" Ian asked.

"Hardly." They were former colleagues, from before she'd been demoted for failing to find the Book of Worlds. Their open disdain was a fact of life now, and she despised it. But she was a *Failte*, one who'd failed her fate, and she should expect it.

She shook the thought away and glanced at Ian out of the corner of her eye, struck once again by the sheer physicality of him. He was so damn big. Three or four inches over six feet. Nearly a foot taller than her and all hard muscle.

When she'd stood so close to him and snapped the collar about his neck, it had been as if a live wire had connected them. She'd wanted to touch him, to see if he felt as hard as he looked.

She shook the thought away. It was crazy. *She* was crazy. She shouldn't be attracted to the too-handsome, black-haired thief whose dark eyes gleamed with intelligence and cunning.

He was a thief, for gods' sake. And not just any kind. A thief of history, of the artifacts she held so dear and had based her life around. They'd barely spoken back in his cell, yet her stupid body was still attracted to him.

Her body was a moron.

"Here we are," she said as they reached her car.

He slid in after her. He filled the small space, his scent dark and masculine.

She swallowed hard. Dealing with him was going to be a whole lot more complex than she'd anticipated.

Ian ran a big hand over the dash. The dials looked minuscule next to his big fingers. "Things have changed."

She laughed. She'd forgotten that he'd been in prison since 1916. "Aye. This car is nothing special, either. Wait 'til you see some of the really nice ones."

He huffed out a laugh and she had to wonder what it was like to see things through his eyes. The university campus wasn't a shock. All rolling hills and oak trees, there were no masses of paved highways here. The buildings were stone monstrosities and were older than he was, so they wouldn't be a shock either.

"We're going to meet Logan." She hadn't mentioned that to Lea when she'd begged for Ian's release. Logan had wanted to ensure she had a way to get into the museum—Ian—before he gave her any more intel. She had a feeling there was more between Logan and Ian than was on the surface, but she was willing to take the risk. She could protect herself, even if it was dangerous as hell to meet a known thief like Logan away from the safety of the Immortal University. It was a risk she was willing to take. She'd reached the end of her line long before this. When Logan, a thief she'd been looking for because he'd stolen from the university, had approached her with information about the book, she'd been skeptical.

But she needed to find that book so damned badly that she'd decided trusting him was worth the risk. It was the only good clue she'd had in over a year.

She pulled the car out of the lot and headed down the lane that led to the university entrance.

Great oaks rose on either side as they rolled down the main drive and arrived at a great wrought iron gate that hid the campus from mortal eyes. It swung open silently, and she drove through the forest that would lead to the main road.

The night was black as tar as they sped down the winding country road, the beam of the headlights cutting through the dark. There were no other cars, and when Fiona pulled onto a lane that led deeper into the forest, if she hadn't known better, she'd think left the last of civilization behind.

"You work for the university, do you no'?" Ian asked.

"Aye."

The Immortal University, which had begun its existence thousands of years ago as a group of Mythean warriors and their families who'd banded together for protection from mortals, had eventually become a research institution of enormous power. Though it had taken the name Immortal University and taught a few classes to educate young Mytheans, the institution was more concerned with ensuring peace between the gods in the afterworlds and mortals on earth. They were keepers and enforcers of Mythean law.

"You're a diplomat?" he asked.

Diplomacy and knowledge were the university's primary tools. But that didn't mean they didn't have a top-notch security division. It was how Ian had ended up imprisoned for his crimes.

"I'm an Acquirer with the Department of Magical Devices." She was a Historius, like him. Their long-dead ancestors had been disciples of the Celtic god Gwydion, a god of magic and the arts, who'd gifted his followers with the ability to locate valuable artwork and artifacts. The skill had passed down through the generations, which were few, as immortals rarely reproduced.

The car turned into the little gravel parking lot at the side of an old country pub.

"Bit remote," Ian said.

"Aye. And better for it." She cut the lights and pulled the key from the ignition.

He followed her up to the heavy wooden door.

"After you," she said as she pushed it open.

He reached over her head so that he held open the door and nodded, indicating she should precede him.

"After you," she repeated, determined not to let him pull that archaic crap on her.

He shook his head, his face set. He wasn't going to move, that much was clear. Stubborn man. She shrugged and walked through because it was easier.

Ian followed Fiona into the pub, his entire body tingling with the glorious sensation of being free. The collar, though a pain in the arse, was nothing compared to the hell he'd just escaped. The air was sweeter, the sky higher, and everything around him more incredible than he'd ever realized.

The pub was dimly lit and dingy, but even that was a joy. A grizzled old barkeep wiped the nicked expanse of wood with a rag and watched them with a frown. The pub was old enough that it reminded him of the pubs of his day, and a rush of nostalgia washed over him.

He'd make this freedom permanent. *Nothing* would stand in his way now that he was out.

He glanced around and caught sight of Logan sitting at a table in the darkest shadows, half his face obscured. A grin stretched across his face and he nodded. Damn, it was good to see his old friend. He turned and followed Fiona to the bar, not wanting to alert her to his familiarity with Logan, though he was certain that she was suspicious.

"Pint of Tennent's," she told the barkeep, then looked at Ian.

He nodded. She drummed her fingers on the bar, no doubt anxious to get the information she sought. But they were in a mortal pub, and blending in was vital.

Fiona handed over two bills after the barkeep set the pints on the bar. The pub was so dingy that even the golden liquid lacked its usual gleam.

They each grabbed a pint, then strode toward Logan, who surveyed them as they approached, his black eyes falcon sharp. His dark hair and pale skin hadn't changed, but the shadows under his eyes were deeper. Ian wanted to hug him and punch him. He'd missed his friend, but damn, he'd expected Logan to get him out of prison sooner.

"It didn't take you long to get him out," Logan said to Fiona. He didn't look at Ian.

"Nay. You were verra convincing this morning. And doona bother pretending you doona know him. There's something between you two," Fiona said.

Logan shrugged. "You're brave, then, if you've come here believing that Ian MacKenzie and I are in league together. One of you against two of us."

"Desperate," Fiona said. "And I can protect myself."

"That, I am aware of. You've been quite aggressive in your hunt for the Book of Worlds."

"Exactly. Desperate enough to be dangerous. I've hunted that book for ten years. I should have found it years ago, and I'm running out of time. It's the only reason I'm taking this chance."

"Ironic, isn't it, that you were hunting me for the theft of the amulet, yet I came to you with something you want even more?" Logan asked.

Amulet? Ian wanted to ask, but Fiona spoke.

"Aye. It's makes me nervous. You didn't give me time to ask this morning, but I assume that in exchange for giving me information about the book, you want me to forget you have the amulet?"

"Exactly. You're tenacious. The last thing I want is the university on my trail for something like the amulet."

Of course he wouldn't want the university knowing much about him, Ian thought. Not with his secrets.

Fiona scowled, then nodded. "Tell me about the book. I'll forget you have the amulet."

"Excellent." Logan said.

"Good. Tell me why the hell the book is in a human museum." Fiona asked. "It shouldn't be there."

"I put it there."

Well, that was unexpected, Ian thought.

"*What?*" Fiona nearly shrieked.

"I bartered it to a god. He had something I wanted. We agreed to drop off our items at neutral locations to make the trade. Except, I didn't pick a neutral location."

"Why?" Fiona's voice was breathless with fear, as if she knew what was coming.

"I'm betting that the god wants to destroy the covenant and reignite the Divine War," Logan said. "I don't want that to happen. I quite like earth the way it is. But I wanted what he had to trade more. So I'm giving the university—and you—a chance to recover the book first. With his help." Logan nodded at Ian.

Ian tipped his head back slightly. *Good man, Logan.* Cunning, as always. Ian had no doubt that Logan spoke the truth. It was precisely like him. Self-interested, yet if given the opportunity, he leaned toward doing right. He'd deny it, but it was in his nature. Seeing that the covenant was in safe hands at the university made sense. Ian might hate the institution, but it was doubtlessly the best place for the book. Everything about this deal worked out in Logan's favor. As usual.

"You selfish fucking bastard! If the covenant is destroyed, there are at least a dozen ancient pantheons that would take the opportunity to come to earth to war for worshippers." Fiona's voice was horrified.

"True," Logan said. "And the mortals would certainly fight to defend their beliefs. The ancient gods would have mortals fighting in their name. Nothing would please them more after millennia of being ignored."

The idea made Ian's skin crawl. He liked earth the way it was. After all his time in prison, he didn't want to be released into another hell. Not all gods wanted worshippers to war in their name, but many of the most ancient ones did.

"Which god did you trade it to?" Fiona asked. Fiona looked like she was about to reach across the table and strangle Logan.

"I don't know," Logan said.

"How the hell do you no' know?" Fiona's jaw was so tense Ian was afraid she'd pull a muscle.

"I made the deal through a broker. Neither the god nor I want anyone to know what we have."

"Shite," Fiona said.

"You can assume that whoever is trying to get the book doesn't just want it for his library," Logan said.

"So we have to beat the mystery god to the book," Ian said.

Logan nodded. "Whoever it is has no idea the museum is enchanted, so he'll likely send an envoy to recover it. Demons or other rogue Mytheans who don't give a damn about the havoc their actions will wreak. They'll expect to break in and have the book in no longer than it takes to walk through the museum."

Ian nodded. It was a good plan. Not foolproof, as his and Logan's enchantments were no doubt warped after lying fallow and would be difficult even for him to get through, but it was a solid plan. They just had to beat the god's envoys and get the book first. Then Ian could steal it and threaten to destroy it unless Fiona removed his collar.

He wouldn't have a chance to speak privately to Logan, but it was clear this was his friend's way of getting him out of the university prison.

Not bad. Not bad at all.

CHAPTER THREE

Shite, shite, shite. Fiona hurried out of the pub behind Ian, Logan's pronouncement sending her heart into overdrive.

"There's a hell of a lot more at stake than I expected," Ian said as he squeezed into her little car.

Life as we know it. But she couldn't find her voice as she cranked the key in the ignition. She'd hoped it wouldn't be so dire. That she could just get into the museum and take it. "I'm going to have to warn the university. *Damn it.*"

"Why?"

"It's too damn risky. We'll do our best to get it, but if we fail, there needs to be backup. But it'll take them time to put together a team."

"You really think that's neccessary?"

"You heard what he said in there. I want that book"—her voice shook—"but no' enough to risk divine war if I fail. They need to at least know about it."

"Why do you want it so badly?" Ian asked as they peeled out of the lot and headed down the road back toward the university and Edinburgh beyond.

"Ten years ago, it was prophesied that I would be the one to find the Book of Worlds. It's been lost for so long, and I was the chosen one. Fated to find the Book of Worlds and bring it back to safe hands at the university. But I never found it. Everywhere I looked, everything I tried—none of it worked. Dead-end after dead-end. It's unheard of for an Acquirer. It's been years since I was supposed to find it. I'm a *Failte*." One who'd failed her fate. Not only had the failure gotten her blacklisted at her job because she was an Acquirer who couldn't find things, she carried the same ugly title that her father had carried. They'd once been an illustrious family of Acquirers, until he'd gone mad after failing his fate. She blinked hard to erase the memories of the past and bring the dark road into focus. "This is my only chance to get the book back and prove that I dinna fail my fate. If I doona, I'll go mad like my father."

"Shite."

"Exactly." Fate was everything in their world. Failing hers meant that she'd eventually go insane, because her subconscious would continually be trying to fulfill her destiny. "My father could no' find the sword of St. Eidyn, and it eventually drove him mad, as it does to all *Failtes*. It ruined our family name. He ended up stealing the artifacts he was supposed to be handing over to the university and hoarding them. Eventually they threw him in prison because they could no' control him. I'm the same. The worst kind of failure."

"No' for long."

She shot him an appraising glance. All of a sudden, she quite liked him. And he was right. This would be her redemption. The university thought her fate was played out. That she'd tried to fulfill it and failed.

They were wrong. The chance she'd been waiting for, searching for, was finally here. She was going to get her old life back. Before she went insane in this one.

"We're heading into town," Fiona said. "I've rented us a flat across from the museum. Just a holiday place for short-term lets. I expected us to have more time to do this. To plan our entry to the museum." She'd even hired a cat-sitter for Fluffy Black, her cat. Now it looked like they'd have to go in tonight.

Her phone shrieked, and she jumped. She fished it out of her pocket and glanced at the screen.

Her stomach dropped to her feet. *Darrence.* Her boss. Had Cerus and Francis told him they'd seen her near the prison? Shite. She could be fired for this if they caught her before she retrieved the book. Retrieving it would give her a *get out of jail free* card. But not retrieving it? She'd lose the job she was so desperately fighting for. Worse, if they stopped her, she'd lose the opportunity to be the one to find the book and save her sanity.

With a shaky hand, she mashed the *End* button and returned her attention to the road.

"I'm going to call Lea." She pushed buttons on her little phone while glancing up occasionally. "Lea? This problem with the Book of Worlds is worse than we thought."

Ian listened with half an ear as Fiona explained to Lea what Logan had told them. The telephone she used was so tiny—even odder, it had no wires connecting it to anything.

He shook his head. The world had changed very much indeed.

While Fiona talked on her tiny phone, he looked around the vehicle, noticing anew how modern and small the car was. He was so close to her he could smell her soap, clean and fresh and very suited to her no-nonsense personality.

The car sped through the dark night, and he marveled at freedom. And how different the world was, though he'd barely seen any of it. He needed the book to bargain with if he wanted to make this permanent. But when she'd said that she was the worst kind of failure, he'd been dumb enough to say *no' for long*. If he stole the book from her, he'd be screwing her. And he liked her. Damn it.

But he didn't have a choice. The thought hardened his resolve.

As they drove, the country road turned to suburb and then to city street. Suddenly, there were flashes of dozens— no, hundreds—of lights hitting him in the face.

"Jesus," he breathed. Cars streamed by on the other side of the road. Nothing at the university or the pub—besides the cars—had looked terribly different than it had in 1916. But Edinburgh…

Fiona continued to talk into the phone while she swerved in and out of traffic. Ian's eyes ate up the changes to Edinburgh as she neared Old Town. His gut clenched at the sight of the familiar old buildings.

He'd made a point to stay out of this part of town once he'd escaped it as a child. The construction of the Scottish Museum of Antiquities in the early nineteenth century had been the only thing that could drag him back, but only for brief visits to add to his collection.

Fiona dropped her little phone into her lap and said, "Right. Lea said that she has to alert the rest of the university to the fact that a god is after the book." She swerved to the side of the road and tucked her car neatly into the little space between a lorry and a motorbike. The museum rose tall on the other side of the street. "Here we are."

"What's your plan then?" he asked when they got out of the car. He sucked in the cold winter air. Even city air tasted fresher than the air of the prison or Moloch. He wanted to tear the collar off and disappear down the street.

"Try to get it before they do. It'll take at least a day for them to compile a team. *I* want to be the one to find the book. I have to be. I did what's right and told them about it, but my department thinks I'm a failure and a jinx because I'm a *Failte*. They doona trust me to go after it and would yank me off this case and shove me back into the stacks. So we go in tonight."

"I like how you think." Less supervision by the university meant he'd have no trouble snatching the book from her and bartering for the removal of his collar. He stifled the twinge of guilt he felt at putting her in such a shite situation. But it had to be done.

He followed her across the rain-darkened sidewalk toward the brick building that loomed in front of them. People rushed by on their way to pubs or home, but it felt like he and Fiona were an island unto themselves. After so long in prison, he craved the intimacy of that connection as much as he feared it.

Damn it. He couldn't let her distract him.

Ian followed Fiona up the stairs, his gaze riveted to her form and the trousers that molded to it. Christ, the way women dressed these days. The way the clothes moved on her body, clinging to curves and muscles, sent a jolt of lust through him. His palms itched to touch her. With an internal curse, he dragged his eyes away.

He'd done everything he could to keep from turning into an animal in prison. No way he was going to let some tight trousers turn him into a slavering beast now that he was free.

I am no' an animal, damn it.

But damned if she didn't make him feel like one. He'd been going mad in prison, driven insane by the misery of repetition and constant toil. The lack of freedom to decide his fate had been nearly unbearable. Then she'd opened the door and let in the light. She'd led him out. Of course he couldn't keep his mind off her.

Finally, they reached the top floor and Fiona unlocked the door to flat 7A. It swung open and they entered the small space.

Ian glanced around. Kitchen and living room combination on one side and a small hall that led to a bath and two bedrooms on the other side. The kitchen was strange as hell and vastly different from the ones he'd seen before. There was a low hum of the electric appliances. The prison had electric lights, but other than that, not much had changed there since he'd been incarcerated.

"No' bad for a base," Fiona said and dropped her bag onto the couch.

Though the hum of the appliances was unsettling, he liked how different it was from the prison. He could get used to modern conveniences. He followed her to the window. The view of the huge, ornate building that housed the

Scottish Museum of Antiquities made his blood run faster. His fists clenched like a junkie's in need of a fix.

He'd missed the rush of thieving while he'd been in prison, more than he'd ever expected. It was the thrill that had sent him back to it time and again, even after his fortune had grown ridiculously large. On the black market, it took time to turn artifacts into money. Eventually he'd had such a backlog of artifacts that he knew he'd never need to steal again. Added to what he had in the banks, stealing was just an unnecessary risk.

But he'd done it all the same. For the love of it. For the security his fortune brought him. His wealth kept him comfortable in the knowledge that he'd never have to return to his roots. Except he had, in a way. He'd been thrown into prison, and it had been worse than anything he'd suffered as a boy.

He scowled at the memory. "We'll go now. It's after ten. The back alley should be empty at this hour."

"Agreed." She walked to the bag she'd brought, pulled out two long daggers, and slipped them into sheaths that had been built into her tall boots. She shoved a small leather case into the pocket of her jacket.

"Do you have another?" he asked.

She raised a brow. "You expect me to give you a weapon? You're a criminal."

"I'm good with a knife, lassie. If we run into the rogue gods or his demons, you're going to want me at your back."

Her cool gray eyes assessed him. "Fine. I have a spare."

She dug another sheathed knife out of the bottom of her bag and handed it over. It was identical to the ones she'd slipped into her boots. It seemed Fiona liked to be prepared.

He put it into the pocket of his jacket and asked, "Do you have lockpicks?"

She gave him a *don't be an idiot* look and patted her jacket pocket.

"Good." He followed her out the door and down the stairs, his eyes glued to her arse. After so long alone in that miserable prison, his cock hardened just looking at her. Hell, all the protestations in the world that he wasn't an animal wouldn't keep his eyes in check around Fiona.

They slipped out into the cold January air. Biting wind cut through the black night. The museum loomed across the street, an ornate gargoyle of a building that contained the treasures of the ages. Anticipation and a sense of endless possibility zipped through him. The museum, his for the taking. A battle of wit and wills that he would win.

He was free of that damned prison.

Though obnoxious, the collar was nothing compared to the cell. To the lack of control he'd had over his life. But that was about to change. He'd get the book and use it to barter for his freedom. The university couldn't be trusted to spit on you if you were on fire. They sure as hell wouldn't free him when this was all over.

"This way." Fiona set off across the street and he followed.

Noise from the pubs spilled out into the street, and darkened storefronts watched them silently. Gleaming streetlamps marched their way down the sidewalk and cut through the dark night.

Instead of approaching the grand museum entrance on the left, they turned right, toward the alley. Ian took the lead, pleased that Edinburgh hadn't changed much since he'd last been free. A few tourist shops now dotted the first floors of the towering old buildings between the pubs and shops, but the layout was the same.

They dodged a group of drunken lads stumbling to the next pub and turned into the alley. The light dropped instantly, a black gloom overtaking the narrow cobbled space.

"Come on, the door is at the back," he said.

They crept along, their footsteps silent, and he couldn't help but be impressed by Fiona's stealth. She was an Acquirer, basically a thief who had permission to steal, so she would be good at sneaking about. Shame she never kept what she found. Too many morals or something.

A rustling noise made the back of Ian's neck prickle. He stopped, and Fiona pulled to a halt behind him. His muscles tensed as he waited for another sound.

There. Another rustle. Had the god's envoys beaten them to the museum? Fiona stepped forward. He reached behind and pressed a hand to her stomach, staying her. He couldn't help the shiver that ran up his arm at the feel of her soft warmth beneath his palm.

A moan filtered through the alley and Fiona tensed beneath his hand. He barely perceived her reaching into her boot to withdraw her dagger.

The moan sounded again, this time louder and clearer. His gaze snapped toward the sound and he saw two figures pressed against the wall near the museum's small private entrance.

Holy fuck. Two people were having sex. His blood rushed even as annoyance surged through him. Had he not been locked up for nearly a century, no doubt he'd have only felt annoyance.

He stepped forward to break up the party, but Fiona's hand clamped on his arm.

"Nay," she hissed. "I doona want them knowing our faces."

He turned back. "What?"

"In case something goes wrong at the museum. I doona want a trail that leads back to us. Come on." She pulled his arm. "We'll wait it out in this doorway."

His jaw clenched, but he let her lead him toward an inset doorway. They had about two feet of cubbyhole in which to hide, so he stepped onto the stoop behind her and tucked himself into the shadows. They stood so close together that he could feel the heat of her against him.

He stiffened, unable to keep his cock from following suit. It'd been too damn long.

The noises from the alley increased. Damn drunken idiots.

Fiona whispered from behind him, "You're a Historious. Why'd you turn to stealing? You could have worked for the university as an Acquirer, like me."

His head whipped around. "What?"

"I doona get it. You could have had a nice life and never gotten arrested." She sounded genuinely perplexed.

He sure as hell could use a distraction from the couple in the alley, so he answered. "The only way to get a nice life is to build it for yourself. No way in hell was the university going to get it for me."

"Why no'? You've got the skills. They'd have hired you."

"I'm no' a joiner. I grew up on the streets of Edinburgh, a half-breed Mythean orphan who had no one and nothing."

"You never knew who your parents were?"

"Nay. It took me years to figure out there were others like me, and years more to piece together that I'm half Sylph and half Historius." It'd taken years of research to figure out he'd gotten his invisibility from his Sylph parent, and a bloodhound's sense for the location of valuable artifacts from his Historious parent. The ability to work spells had come shortly after he'd frozen into his immortality around thirty. But who his parents were, he had no idea.

"I'm sorry."

"Doona be."

"So you turned out to be a thief," she said. "You use your powers to steal history."

Cold pierced him and he felt a pinch in his chest. Confused, he rubbed over his heart. "You doona like that."

"No' too fond of it."

"I only stole from those who could afford it." He found that he wanted her to think well of him. It felt weird as hell to care what anyone else thought, especially someone from the university.

"I doona know that I agree with that. You specialized in ancient artifacts, right?"

"Aye. Their owners were dead. What did they care?" The noise from the couple in the alley picked up, and he tried to focus on Fiona. It wasn't difficult. She smelled so damn good.

"Maybe so. But ancient artifacts belong in museums, to the descendants of those who'd made them. To modern people who can learn from them. They're our past, evidence of where we've come from. They shouldn't be hidden away by wealthy individuals who can afford to buy them on the black market." Though she whispered, passion rang in her voice. She really believed this stuff. She had a commitment to something bigger than herself.

He'd never had that, personally. Hadn't had the luxury. But he liked that she had it. Liked that she gave him a piece of her mind, too.

"Sounds lovely on paper," he said. "But when there's nothing between a person and the poorhouse, it becomes exceedingly easy to nick something from people who've been dead for centuries."

"There are other ways to survive."

"Aye, for some. For a Mythean orphan on his own who has the mortal workhouse at his back? Why shouldn't he use his skills to the best of his advantage? No one else is going to care for him." The words flowed out on a tidal wave of repressed anger. He blinked in shock.

He'd never shared his past before, not when it was so ugly and unflattering. Though Logan was his only true friend in the world, he hadn't even shared it with him.

"I'm sorry. That's awful." Sincerity rang in her voice.

Heat threatened to creep up his neck, an unfamiliar and unwelcome sensation. "Aye. But doona pity me. I turned out all right."

His past wasn't anything to be ashamed of, damn it. His childhood had been shite—an unwanted orphan—but he'd made the best of it. He sharpened his gaze on the alley and tried to ignore her at his back. But even the rising sounds of the lovers couldn't drown out Fiona's voice.

"I see your point. I sound like an idealist and a prude. Cultivating and preserving our history is a luxury. Survival is a necessity." Her voice sharpened, and he worried it would alert the mortals. "But I'll be watching you in there. I've got everything on the line here. I'm totally fucked if this goes wrong."

Totally fucked. Gods, the way women talked these days.

He liked it. He liked her, and the fact that she told him exactly how she felt, that she didn't back down and gave as good as she got. True, the fact that she didn't trust him burned. But why should she? She'd been in his prison cell. He wouldn't trust him either.

She'd given him the knife, though. She might not trust him to ignore his thief's ways, but she did have faith in him not to kill her. It was a very basic thing, but it warmed his chest. Which was evidence of how low he'd fallen—he was pleased the woman he wanted didn't think he'd kill her.

"Right, then. No stealing." Except the book.

The moans and rustling of the lovers in the alley cut through his thoughts. His breath tightened in his throat at the images that flashed through his mind. Him and Fiona, in this very corner of the alley. His fists tightened. *Ignore it.* But there was a beast within him that had been caged for far too long.

CHAPTER FOUR

The sounds in the alley were sending streaks of heat through Fiona. Her desperation to find the book had pushed out all other aspects of life. She hadn't been doing nearly enough of what they were doing.

And Ian, who was tense as a wire, was in the same boat. He'd been without sex for nearly a century. *A century*. It almost didn't sound real. She squeezed her eyes shut and tried not to imagine what was happening in the alley. What she could be doing.

Her eyes snapped open. That was crazy. She needed to get her mind on the job.

"Ian, we need to—" She snapped her mouth shut when a rustling from the other end of the alley caught her attention. She whipped her head around and peered into the darkness. Ian did the same.

Nothing. The couple at the other end of the alley suddenly quieted. Tension prickled along Fiona's arms. Was something here with them?

The mortals giggled, then stumbled toward the new noise. Fiona gripped her knife and squinted after them, her skin prickling with awareness.

But the mortals passed unharmed onto the street and went on their way.

Fiona shook away the eerie feeling and followed Ian deeper into the alley. The back door to the museum was made of unmarked steel. The lock at the door, however, was familiar.

"Keep an eye out." She knelt in front of the door.

"I'll take care of it." Ian reached for the little leather pack of tools she'd withdrawn from her coat pocket.

She yanked them away. "I've got it. And this is a way newer lock than you've ever tried to pick."

"Natural skill." The cockiness in his tone made her grit her teeth, but he turned and covered her while she made the lock give up its secrets.

She felt the latch give and stood with a grin. Anticipation sang in her veins. "We're in."

Ian turned to her. "Good work, we'll be—"

A shadow loomed behind Ian, then two arms reached out and picked him up, throwing him into the wall. Fiona stifled a scream as she yanked a knife out of her boot and flung it at the hulking figure. Shadow hid its features, but its bellow was unmistakable. Her knife had found its mark.

She didn't have time to spare a glance for Ian as she yanked the other knife free of her boot. Before she could throw it, the figure was upon her, knocking the blade from her fist and wrapping meaty hands around her neck.

She gasped and kicked as he hoisted her into the air. She caught sight of an eerie face—snub nose, slitted eyes, and long fangs—and kicked harder. Her throat throbbed and she clawed at the demon's hands. Black spots danced in front of her eyes. Shite, she was going to pass out. She didn't know what kind of demon he was, but she'd be dead in seconds if she fell unconscious.

Suddenly, the hands released her and she hit the ground hard, toppling to her arse. At her feet, Ian was wailing on the demon, his fists a blur as he beat her attacker's face.

Ian plucked the blade from his pocket and raised it.

"Doona!" Fiona reached out for him. "We need to—"

The blade sliced down, straight through the attacker's neck. Ian put such force behind the cut that he severed the throat to the spine. Another hard hack and the spine was gone too.

She collapsed back onto her butt. "Shite."

Ian dropped the now-dead demon and knelt at her side. Rage and worry fought in his eyes. "Are you all right?"

She coughed. "Fine, but we needed to find out where he came from!"

Ian scowled. "Bloody bastard was going to snap your neck."

"I was fine!" She hadn't been, but she was so peeved she didn't care.

"Really?" Concern radiated from him despite his glare.

Something twitched in her chest. She had a protector. She'd never had one of those before. It was problematic, considering that they needed to know who the demon worked for, but it was quite nice, really. Annoying. But nice.

"I'm fine." She glanced at the demon. He'd begun to steam. "Move it, I need a picture."

She crawled away from Ian and yanked out her phone to take a quick picture of the demon's sublimating face. Eventually, he'd reappear in the hell from which he came.

"What the hell was that for?" Ian asked.

She turned to snap at him, but shut her mouth when police sirens rang through the night.

"Damn it! The alarm." She grabbed Ian's hand and pulled. "We need to get out of here. The demon distracted me before I could stop the museum's alarm system. It alerted the police."

"Fuck." Ian surged to his feet.

Fiona reached for the door and locked it, then pushed it closed. Mortals didn't have her prints on file, so she paid no mind to shielding her hands.

She jumped over the remains of the demon, who'd almost entirely disappeared, and ran down the alley with Ian. They reached the main street.

Thank gods, no police yet.

"Wrap your arm around my shoulder," she said. "And pretend you're pissed."

He did as she said, and they stumbled off down the street as if they'd just been to the pub. Fortunately, there were so many around here that it wouldn't look strange. They were slipping into the doorway of the building that housed their flat when the first police car pulled to a stop in front of the museum.

"Damn it, Ian," she said as they climbed the stairs to the flat. "We needed to find out who that demon worked for. Logan will no' tell us, but I want to know which god is after the book. Why'd you have to kill him?"

"You expect me no' to kill him after I watch him try to strangle the life from you?" The residual violence in his voice sent a shiver down her spine. It was weird, but she kind of liked it. Though it *had* screwed them.

"I bet that the god who wants the book sent only one demon to get it, because he thought it would be an easy grab job. When that one does no' show up with the book, he'll just send more."

"No' killing him would no' have changed that."

"True. But I wanted to question him."

"I'll no' kill the next one, how about that?"

She scowled. "The police are going to be canvassing the museum all night. They'll want to make sure no one got in."

"Then we canna go back in until tomorrow. Though the mortal police will no' trigger the enchanted exhibits, our presence would. I can navigate around them, but it might no' be a quiet job."

"Fine. The god will no' realize his demon has failed for a while yet, anyway. We'll go in tomorrow night." She glanced over to see that one of his fists was clenched while the other was pressed to his ribs. And he was limping. "You're hurt."

"He was a bloody big demon who packed a hell of a punch. I'll be fine soon."

She let them into the flat and turned to him. "Take off your jacket."

His brows rose.

"I just want to check your ribs. You've been favoring them." Gods, some weird, crazy compulsion had her wanting to take care of him. Nothing crazy, like washing his clothes, but check out his wounds at least. Besides popping the top on

Fluffy's Meowy Meal cans, she wasn't really a caretaker. But she wanted to take care of him. She scowled.

"Well?" she asked.

He gave her a long look, then shrugged out of his jacket and drew the shirt up over his head. His arms dropped and he gripped the cotton loosely in his right fist.

She sucked in a breath at the sight of rigid muscles, then coughed, trying to cover the noise. *Smooth.* Broad chest and trim hips created a proportion that the ancient Greeks would have envied. Pythagoras would have discovered a golden triangle had he seen Ian.

"Move your arm." She tried her damnedest to make her voice brisk, but the huskiness was plain even to her ears.

She walked to him and ran her fingers lightly over the bruise on his ribs, searching for a broken bone.

He hissed in a breath at her touch, but she swore it wasn't a sound of pain. He stiffened as her fingers ran over his smooth skin and she was dreadfully, wonderfully aware of his gaze on her. It burned through her, from her scalp to her ankles, lingering at the more interesting bits in between.

With her fingertips pressed to his warm skin, she glanced up. Her breath caught at the look in Ian's eyes.

Hunger. It cut through the exhaustion that had built up and hit her right in the chest, along with the reality of it all. She was in a tiny flat with a criminal. A man who hadn't been with a woman in a century. The idea made her hot and cold at once.

She shook her head. Nerves over finding the book were making her jittery.

Liar. Nerves weren't the only thing making her jittery. He made her jittery. The way he watched her made her jittery. No one had looked at her that way in years, or if they had, she'd had her nose so far in a book she hadn't noticed.

His dark eyes never strayed from her face, never moved south to the parts she was sure he'd dreamed about in prison, all alone in his cell. The idea made her mind buzz. She *wanted* his gaze to stray. The idea made her hot, made dirty images flash through her mind like a magazine that should be shoved under a mattress.

This was the best opportunity she had to get the book back. Her career depended on this. Weird fantasies would get her nowhere.

She stepped back. "Well, your ribs are fine."

He nodded.

"So, um… It's getting late. Probably time for bed." She was babbling. She knew she was, but she couldn't help it.

"I assume I'm sleeping here?"

"Aye. There're two bedrooms."

"Thanks." He glanced down, then back up, uncertainty drawing his brows together. The uncertainty was strange on such a big man—one who could fight like a warlord. Broad shoulders, forearms roped with muscles and those sexy veins that popped, big hands that hung at his sides. "You doona have to worry about me, you know."

"What?" She flushed.

"You're a woman alone and you doona know me. But we're sharing a flat. I understand that you're nervous, but you doona have to be. I'll respect your boundaries. Stay right away from you." He looked like he was worried he might scare her off.

"Oh. I— thank you." And suddenly she was no longer jittery. Not from fear, at least. "Um, I'm going to hit the hay. But there's TV if it's still early for you."

"TV?"

"Oh, shite. I'm sorry. Could you watch TV in prison?" The enormous differences between their lives loomed in the tiny space between them. Not only was he out of prison for the first time in nearly a century, it was the twenty-first century. But there was no leeway in their schedule for him to adjust to the outside world.

"I doona even know what it is."

"Crap. Uh, I'll show you some other time. Sorry."

"Doona be. You keep saying that, but doona be. I sure as hell doona like that you work for the university, but quit saying you're sorry."

She nodded. Her apologies were so futile. There was no way she could understand it. Or him. But she wanted to. She didn't want to analyze why, when she hadn't cared enough to try to understand any other guy in years. But she wanted to understand him. "What did you do for all that time in prison?"

His eyes darkened. "I spent an eternity doing forced labor in a hellish afterworld, constructing a monstrosity of a cathedral in the middle of an abandoned hell. In the midst of hundred-degree heatwinds and smoldering embers, I worked for nearly a hundred fucking years creating something in hell that was constantly destroyed before my eyes."

Horror carved a hole in her chest. "What? Why?"

"I've no idea. The university wanted something built, and prisoners are good labor. It kept us too tired to cause trouble at the end of the day. But it was hell." His fists clenched at his sides.

Fiona's heart ached for him, for what she imagined it must have been like. She loved the university and truly believed that it was a foundation of good in their world. They worked hard to protect mortals and Mytheans alike. But they were an ancient institution. Using prisoners as forced labor wasn't at all strange to those who ran the university.

Most of the elders who ran the place were ancient. She was far younger—a mere thirty-six chronologically, though she'd stopped physically aging sometime in her mid-twenties. An infant to Mytheans. She had modern ideals about ethics that many at the university lacked. For the most part, the prisoners were truly evil. Ian wasn't, but hearing his story made her want to fight harder to drag the university into the twenty-first century.

Guilt streaked through her at the knowledge that she'd lied to him about the university possibly releasing him if he helped her retrieve the book. She'd needed his help so badly—to preserve her very sanity and her life—that she'd have said anything to get him to help. But that was before she'd realized that she liked him. And now she'd have to send him back to that hell, else risk her own freedom. Permanently releasing a dangerous prisoner could get her in *serious* trouble.

Gods, this was all too complicated. She needed some space. "I'm headed to bed."

"All right. I'm going to get cleaned up in the bathroom and do the same."

"Do you know how to work the shower?"

"I'll figure it out."

She nodded, then spun and walked toward the little hallway that led to the bedrooms, grabbing her bag on the way.

As soon as she was in the tiny room, an image of Ian in the shower flashed in her mind. She rubbed a hand over her forehead, trying to banish the thought. There was a hell of a lot more complexity to this situation than she'd planned on.

She liked him. And boy, did she want him.

Wow, celibacy was so easy when there was no one around to tempt a person. His presence in her normally bare and boring life was so out of the ordinary it was like she now inhabited a different life entirely.

She tried not to think about all the things that work had evicted from her life. Like men. Like sex.

Those things had no place in her life, not until she found the book. She couldn't afford them. He was here to work for her. And he was a damned thief. This was her best chance at getting the book back, and she couldn't afford to lose her focus.

There was a job to be done. *The* job.

CHAPTER FIVE

Ian shut the bathroom door and leaned against the smooth wood. A great sigh shuddered out of him. Adjusting to the real world was going to be harder than he'd expected.

He turned and braced his hands on the small pedestal sink. A glance in the mirror confirmed it—he barely recognized the man looking out at him.

In prison, it hadn't mattered that he was changing. He'd changed to survive.

Had he expected to return to his old self when he got out? Hell, he didn't know. He didn't even know if he remembered that man.

But he hadn't expected to lose his damned mind over a university Acquirer. He didn't want to like her. He didn't want to want her. She worked for the organization that had thrown him in prison and tortured him for nearly a hundred years. She would throw him back in again when this was all over.

His mind should be on getting the book in order to barter his way out of this collar. Instead, his thoughts were on the woman who'd sprung him from hell—and it pissed him off.

Maybe he liked her because she was the first woman he'd seen in a century. Or hell, maybe it was because she was nice to convicts and worried about his ribs and was passionate about her work and wasn't afraid to speak her mind.

Shite, he'd turned into a sap. Being so close to her all night, trying to keep the nature of his thoughts hidden, had been hard as hell. When she'd called lights out, he'd thanked the gods, if only to have a chance to hide the damn hard-on that wouldn't go down.

Ian pushed away from the sink and turned on the shower. His clothes hit the floor seconds later, and he was under the cold spray before it could heat up. When the cold water did nothing for his erection, he reached down to grip himself. He was hard and heavy and *fuck*, it felt good.

"Gods damn it," he muttered.

He couldn't jerk off in the damn shower he shared with her. It was fucking barbaric and a shitty way to thank her for getting him out of prison. He squeezed hard, punishing, then let go with a groan. He touched the collar around his neck, reminding himself of where he stood with her.

He let the spray pound down on him and tried to get his mind off Fiona. He forced himself to remember what being trapped in that damned prison had felt like. It wasn't hard. Hell, he'd been out only a few hours. Except the memories highlighted the contrast between where he'd been and where he was now.

It wasn't the damn lust or the insistent fucking hard-on for Fiona that bothered him the most. No, it was the fact that it felt so damn good just to be with her on the outside, like a normal gods-damned Mythean. When prison sucked your soul out and wrung you dry, freedom felt like the best thing in the world.

He'd never wanted that closeness, that casual comfort in his first life. He'd been living it up. Young and stupid and careless. First struggling to survive, then so wealthy he hadn't known what to do with the money besides spend it on women and fucking Model T's.

Model T's. Jesus. That's how long ago it had been, and prison had made him realize how little he cared about that bullshite now.

He turned off the shower and scrubbed a towel over his skin. He had to keep his act together, do this job for Fiona, and get this collar the hell off. Finding the book was the best way to do it.

Scowling, he glanced around for his duffel bag. Damn it. He'd left it out in the living room. Fiona was in her bedroom now, so it was probably safe to run out there. He wrapped the towel around his waist and opened the door.

He stepped out into the tiny hall and right into Fiona. Who looked fucking gorgeous.

Of course.

"Oh!" Her back hit the wall and she stared up at him, lips slightly parted.

They were so damn close he could see her eyelashes, spiky and dark and framing steel-gray eyes that raced over his face. The damned hard-on that had dissipated began to spring back to life. He stepped back, reached to secure his towel.

Oh fuck, she looked good. She was wearing some kind of huge T-shirt. It was ugly and old and so soft that it floated over her curves until it stopped above her knees. He'd never seen anything so hot or so exactly perfect, not in his first life, not in his dreams in prison.

He wanted her more than he'd wanted anything in his life. He wanted to push her against the wall and bury his face in her hair. Smell her, taste her. Touch all the soft parts of her that he'd been denied for so long but looked glorious on her.

Doona think about it.

"Sorry. Just getting my bag." His voice was rough.

"Oh, uh, sure. I was going to get some water."

They stared at each other, the air too thin between them, and he tried to keep his eyes on her face. Hers glanced off his naked chest and bounced back to his eyes. Seconds passed and she had every chance to walk away, but instead she kept glancing down at his chest and the towel clutched around his waist.

He knew he should go get his bag. Just as soon as he could tear himself away from her. If she wasn't going to walk away, he should.

"Um, I just realized I haven't asked you if there's anyone you wanted to call. You know. Like a girlfriend?" She bit her lip, eyes worried.

"No one waited for me." And why did she care?

"Oh." Relief flooded her face.

Holy shite, she did care.

Her eyes dropped to his chest again. He felt like the water droplets were going to steam right off of him.

Gods.

His fist tightened on the towel at his waist. He knew damn well it was tented. When her eyes dropped to it, he felt a flush of desire race up his torso and had to bite back a groan.

She bit her lip and yanked her eyes up to his. He swore he saw desire. Or he was fucking imagining things.

"Gods, Fiona, when you look at me like that, it makes it hard to forget how damn beautiful you are." His feet carried him a step toward her, close enough that he could smell her hair and feel her heat in the chilly hallway. "What do you want, Fiona?" he asked. But he knew what she wanted. He could see it in the flush of her cheeks, hear it in the quickness of her breath, smell the heady scent of it on the air.

"I, um…" Her eyes darted down and back up again.

Her gaze was making him crazed, so he leaned in to where he couldn't see it and said at her ear, "I want this, Fiona, so damn bad that I might be misinterpreting your signals. I think you want this too, but I'm going to need to hear it. You want this, you have to say it. If no', then no problem. I'll leave you alone."

She shuddered at the feel of his breath and his cock jerked.

"I, um… I should probably get to bed." She slipped to the side and down the hall, her heavy breaths still punctuating the silence with the sound of her desire.

His fist clenched and he leaned against the wall, propping his forehead on the hard surface and squeezing his eyes closed. He felt like a fist squeezed his cock and his throat unbearably. But he didn't just want a woman. He wanted Fiona. But she didn't want him.

It was going to be a damn long night.

CHAPTER SIX

An incessant beeping noise dragged Ian from a dream of warm skin and a willing woman. He popped upright in bed, muscles tensed and ready for a threat. It took less than a second for him to process his surroundings.

Safe.

For the first time in nearly a century. The beeping noise stopped. It must have been some sort of alarm in Fiona's room. His muscles gradually relaxed, and he climbed out of the bed that felt like heaven. It'd taken him ages to get to sleep, since he was so used to the prison's threadbare, ancient mattress.

But once he had fallen asleep...

Gods, the dreams. So similar to the ones he'd had in prison, yet infinitely better. Because they featured Fiona. He wanted her nearly as badly as he wanted his freedom. He glanced down at his erection and frowned. It was becoming a problem.

He shook the thought away and pulled on his clothes, the same rugged black pants and sweater that he'd worn in prison.

Though the hellish afterworld he worked in had been hot, the prison had been freezing cold. At least the attire was suited to the Scottish winter, and if one looked closely, it didn't appear any different than modern clothing.

Which he supposed it was. The university got their supplies from the outside, even though the prison felt like it was trapped in time.

The sound of water rushing through the pipes echoed through the room. Fiona must be showering. He went out to the living room to wait. He glanced around, taking in the modern furniture. So unfamiliar.

Holy hell, he was free. He had the collar, but still, he was freer than he'd been in nearly a century. It was hard to believe. He touched the metal that had become his cage. The key had been turned by a beautiful, intriguing woman, but it was a cage nonetheless.

A tapping noise at the window drew his attention. He glanced over. A black falcon sat on the sill, tapping the window with its beak.

About time. He strode to the window and pushed it open. The falcon hopped inside, then on a swirl of green light, transformed into a tall, dark-haired man.

"Logan." He hugged his friend, grinning. Then hauled back and punched him. Ian didn't give a damn if Logan was actually a god who could smite him with a thought. He wouldn't do it. Logan liked him too much, and it was mutual. Ian had kept Logan's secret ever since he'd learned it years ago: that his friend was Loki, the Norse trickster god who'd been kicked out of his afterworld centuries ago. He'd been living in secret as a Mythean of indeterminate species named Logan, and Ian would see to it that the secret was kept. Logan was a shapeshifter, which made it fairly easy to maintain a false identity.

They'd met when Ian had saved Logan's life nearly two hundred years ago. Ian had been attempting to rob an Egyptian tomb and had come upon Logan in the central chamber. The man had been caught within the wind of time, an enchantment meant to protect the tomb's contents. Time accelerated within the wind; it should have caused time to pass so quickly that Logan would die within seconds. Ian had used his Sylph's ability to control the air to halt the wind and had learned that Logan had been trapped there for years, unable to die because he was a god.

Ian had kept the secret of Logan's true identity, revealed because Logan couldn't maintain his illusions within the wind. They'd gone on to rob the tomb together, splitting the wealth in the end. They'd been so successful that they'd formed a team, joining up to rob tombs that were too dangerous to attempt alone.

"Damn it," Logan hissed. He rubbed his jaw and glared at Ian. "What the hell was that for?"

"I thought you'd get me out of the university prison sooner, you bastard. And keep it down. Fiona's in the shower."

Logan scowled. "I know. I checked through the window. And I tried to get you out earlier. It's a damn fortress. You're lucky I came up with this plan."

"Aye, thank you. And it's damn good to see you. You have a way to get me out of this collar?" He felt regret over leaving Fiona so soon, but he'd do it in a heartbeat if it meant not having to go back to that hellhole of a prison.

"No. You've got to get the book, like I told Fiona. Use that to barter your way free."

"Damn. That's what I suspected. I doona want to screw her over. Do you no' have another way?"

Logan shook his head. "Everything is falling into place for me. I've got to leave Scotland for a while. I just stopped by to make sure you understood the terms. I can do no more for you. I'm sorry I took so long. I owed you better, friend." Logan grimaced, regret in his gaze.

"I appreciate it now." And he knew how much Logan's endgame meant to him. He liked Ian, but he wouldn't sacrifice it for him, no matter how close they were.

Logan nodded and clapped him on the shoulder. "Get the book back. You can do it."

"Aye, I'll have to."

Logan grinned. "Freedom suits you. Good luck with the book." He nodded his head toward the bathroom. "And good luck with the woman."

Logan shook his hand then disappeared in a swirl of green, flying off in his falcon form over the tops of Edinburgh's buildings.

The bathroom door creaked open. Ian whirled around.

"Morning," Fiona said.

"Morning."

"Why's the window open?"

"Fresh air."

She looked at him like he was crazy. It was freezing out. "All right. I thought we'd go check out the museum. We canna break in to the vault until dark because there are far too many mortals working in the offices in the basement, but it couldn't hurt to refamiliarize yourself with the layout. Your enchantments activate only around Mytheans. Will they activate around us?"

"No' as long as mortals are around. A precaution we put in place."

"We? So you did have a partner. Logan."

Shite. He was letting his guard down around her. She obviously knew something was up between them, had maybe even heard voices out here, but he didn't need to lay the information at her feet.

"I've no idea what you're talking about. Let's go."

She shook her head, as if she knew he was full of shite but didn't care. Her priorities were with the book, not with his past.

It didn't take long for them to gather their coats and hide their daggers. Hers went into the clever sheaths in her boots, his into the lining of his coat. He followed her down the stairs, his gaze riveted to her form.

When they stepped out into the brisk winter air, the hustle and bustle of the street hit him in the face. It was no busier than it had been when he'd lived here before, but it was so damn different. The same ancient buildings rose high into the air, pressed cheek by jowl, along with glass windows that glared down, disapproving of the changes.

Colorful Christmas decorations were strung up all along the street, and cheery music blasted from a storefront nearby. People in brightly colored clothes rushed about, hauling bags of gifts and dodging through traffic, while a man next to him held up a small device and smiled stupidly.

Fiona saw him staring and said, "It's a phone. And a camera. He's taking a picture of the church."

Jesus. Times had changed and there was a hell of a lot he had to learn.

"Let's go get the book." The sooner they did, the sooner he'd be free and could catch up and start a new life.

They stopped at a shop on the way and bought sausage rolls and tea, then crossed the street and climbed the massive stairs that led up to great doors of the museum. He hadn't destroyed this part, at least. Just the west wing.

They spent the next three hours touring the museum, pretending to be like any other couple interested in the paintings, artifacts, skeletons, and models. It was a huge museum, crammed with a bit of everything. It had expanded over the years, new wings added every few decades. The result was a labyrinth of different architectures and styles.

In addition to the small bits and bobs in the display cases, they passed skeletons of mammoths and dinosaurs, mummies, carriages, a variety of cannons, stuffed birds of prey and old costumes on mannequins.

"Can you sense anything about the enchantments you put in place?" Fiona asked.

"Nay. No' until they activate. They may still be good, or time may have warped them. Magic is no' my strong suit." He had nothing compared to the abilities of the witches and soulceresses, just a bit that had been handed down through the generations on his Historius side. It was enough that he could concoct the enchantments, however, especially with Logan's help.

"Damn."

"Aye."

The top floor of the museum was smaller than the rest. They stood alone in a small room at the far back corner. The pottery collection was located next to a door that led to a rooftop balcony. A sign was hung upon it that said *No Trespassing.*

Just what he'd been looking for.

"Come on," he said, pulling on her hand to lead her through the door.

"Is there an entrance up there?"

"Aye, should be. Let's check."

She nodded and followed him through the door. He didn't let go of her hand as he led her up the stairs. He didn't need to hold it. He should release her. She was more than capable of finding her way.

But he didn't let go.

"Does this lead to the roof?" she asked.

"You'll see. It'll be worth it." He'd found it on one of his first visits to the museum, while he'd been casing it to figure out future plans of attack.

They reached the top of the stairs, and he flipped the lock and pushed open the heavy wooden door. Cold wind blasted him in the face as they stepped out onto a small section of the roof. A bell tower loomed over them to their left and cast a shadow over the back of the patio.

"Wow," Fiona breathed.

"Looks like all is good. We can use this entrance tonight if we need to. Come on." Her hand was warm in his as he pulled her over to the edge. A waist-high wall rose up at the edge of the patio.

"This is beautiful. You can see everything." Fiona's voice was tinged with awe.

Ian looked to the left at the extinct volcano that rose up at the edge of town. Arthur's Seat. It was barren and beautiful, the place where Europe's magical energy was the strongest. The university had been built here because of it.

"It's an amazing city," she said. "So full of history. I can feel all of it."

Ian smiled. It was part of being a Historious. The pull of artifacts and history was a comforting feeling. So familiar to his kind, yet foreign to others. Even if stealing artifacts couldn't make him wealthy, he would still hunt them. It was in his blood, like it was in hers.

"We have that in common," he said.

She nodded. "I love the hunt. The search. It's more than just a job. It's my life. I love it. I need it."

"Aye, exactly."

"We'll find the book. We have to." She turned to him. The sight of her, so determined and beautiful, hit him hard in the chest. She glanced up at him and frowned.

He stepped back, realizing that he was staring at her like a starving man.

"We should go," he said.

"Aye." But she didn't move. The expression on her face changed from confusion to something else, something that had her eyes skipping down his body, then back up to his face.

"Fiona." As her name tore from his throat, it dawned on him that she'd stepped forward until she stood nearly toe-to-toe with him.

He had a feeling that she hadn't realized she'd done it. It seemed like her thoughts had turned away from the book, and his were helpless but to follow.

When her hand rose to rest against his chest, he reached down to cup the back of her head. He pulled her to him and pressed his lips to hers. Something like a growl rose in his throat when her lips parted beneath his.

She surged against him, wrapping her strong arms about his neck. The feel of her against him, soft and curved, made his cock throb. The streak of desire was so hot it made him growl low in his throat, then clench his fist in her hair to hold her still for his mouth.

Her tongue met his and all he could think about was lifting her up so that she sat on the half-wall and he could get at the zipper to her jeans. He wanted inside her. Now.

So badly that it scared him.

It felt like he was losing control of his body, the long-denied lusts that had ridden him rising to the fore until they stamped out his conscious thought and possibly her will as well.

That scared him. He tore away from her, mourning the lost taste of her lips but too afraid of where his body might be going without his mind.

She blinked up at him, shiny lips parted and breath coming fast. "Ian, um… I…"

"We should go."

She nodded, seeming to come back to her senses. "Okay. You're right. Of course."

Ian spun from her and headed back to the metal door that led back into the museum. He had no idea how he was going to keep his hands off her now.

Fiona and Ian dodged pedestrians back to their rented flat. The two of them were like water that was just about to burst into a boil. There was no stopping it.

It was surreal to be this close to the book, yet be distracted by a thief who'd stolen the artifacts she'd dedicated her life to finding and protecting.

She couldn't help it; her mind was on the man at her side. "Ian MacKenzie, is that ye?"

Fiona turned around to look at the man they'd just passed. Tall and slender, he was wearing ratty clothes and looking at Ian with recognition gleaming in his buggy eyes. If he recognized Ian, he was a Mythean, not human. He had to be, to still be alive and look so young.

She tensed.

"Tommy MacFee." Ian's voice was reserved as he shifted to stand partially in front of Fiona.

She elbowed him and moved to his side. She could protect herself.

"Who's that ye got there? Lovely bird, she is." His accent was far thicker than hers or Ian's.

Fiona scowled at him.

"You always were an arse, Tommy," Ian said.

"Aye, ye'd know now, would ye no'?" Tommy reached into the pocket of his scrubby jeans and fished out a cigarette and a lighter.

"Goodbye, Tommy." Ian nodded and took her arm.

"Oy, wait." He blew out a puff of smoke. "We're running a con tomorrow night. Could use a hand like yours. Interested?"

"Nay."

"What, too fancy now, are ye? All yer money and yer women and yer standards. Too good for what ye came from? Ye were the best of us, lad. No' a moral in sight and always brought in the biggest haul."

"It's been over a hundred and fifty years, Tommy. I'm gone from that life."

"Ach, ye know I doona see time like that. Come on then, gotta pretty pay day in it fer ye if ye join us. Just an evening's work."

"Nay, Tommy. Goodbye." Ian pulled on her arm until she turned and followed him. He looked back over his shoulder. "Be careful. Stay out of sight of the university."

She glanced back to see Tommy shrug, then amble off down the street.

"Who was that?"

"Old mate. A walker I grew up with."

A walker. She craned her neck around to see if she could catch sight of him again, but he'd disappeared. So that's what he'd meant about not seeing time, and why he'd asked Ian to join him in a con after so many years apart. Walkers could travel back and forth through time. But if they weren't careful—and it didn't look like Tommy was the careful sort—it scrambled their brains until they couldn't quite tell when things had happened. In Tommy's mind, he might have been with Ian yesterday.

"What did you mean, stay out of sight of the university?"

Ian shrugged. "Doona want to see Tommy anymore, but doona want him to end up in prison either."

"You were close?"

"No one was close in our crowd."

"Then why hang out together?"

"No choice. Canna survive on your own on the streets when you're a Mythean orphan."

They reached the wide blue door to the building that housed their rented flat. He pushed it open and waited for her to precede him inside. They climbed the darkened stairwell in silence, but she couldn't get her mind off the thought of Ian as a child, trying to survive on the streets of Edinburgh.

It was dim in the flat, the sun close to setting and no longer shining through the little windows. It was still midafternoon, but the sun set early this time of year. She flipped the lights on and tried to stow her curiosity about Ian. What they had between them—what little it was—couldn't just be sexual attraction if she was worried about his childhood. She liked him. And that was bad. He had to go back to prison when this was all over. There was no other choice.

So she had to stop worrying about him.

But she couldn't help herself from following him over to the window and looking out. Her palms positively itched to wrap around his waist from behind. Crazy thought.

She clenched them and stood next to him, peering out at the near-darkened street below. Though night fell early in December, they'd have to wait until the street quieted down to break in. It had started to rain, a pathetic sort of drizzle that made the yellow lamps glow eerily and the road gleam darkly. A few people rushed out of the rain. But what about the people that had nowhere to go?

That would have been him as a child, in a time that was far harsher than this.

"Will you tell me about it?" she asked.

"About what?"

"What it was like to be alone out there back then. With Tommy and the others."

He sighed and rubbed the back of his neck. "It's a long time past, lassie. Let's no' worry about it."

But she did. She worried about him. She wanted to know if it was as bad as she was imagining it.

"I never knew my mother. And I haven't seen my father in fifteen years," she said.

He looked down at her, brows drawn. The dim streetlight cast a yellow glow on the side of his face. "You're telling me this so that I'll share, too?"

"Maybe," she said. "Maybe I just want to share it. What you decide to say after is up to you."

His hand tightened on the windowsill.

"You know that he lost his mind because he's a *Failte*. He's a shell now. Just a body. I doona visit him anymore because I canna take it." Her throat burned. That would be her one day. Soon, if she didn't recover the book. She said no more. It felt like the words were boulders stuck in her throat.

"Thank you for telling me." His hand still gripped the windowsill, knuckles white. She wanted to touch him, so badly. Instead, she reached out to trace her finger over the grain of the windowsill.

Minutes passed.

His hand shifted and landed over hers, squeezing lightly.

He turned around and leaned against the wall, staring into the small living room. He didn't look like he was seeing anything, though.

"There's no' much to tell, really. I grew up in Edinburgh in the early nineteenth century. Among the mortals."

"How?" she asked. "How'd you end up there? You're a Mythean."

"I was brought up by an old mortal woman until I was five. I knew she wasn't my mother, but I've no idea how I ended up with her. We were hungry and cold almost all the time, but she was kind. For the most part. When she died, her son sold me to the workhouse. A glassworks. It was like a fucking nightmare I'd never wake up from, but I had it no worse than any other child had it in the workhouses. Half of Britain ran on the backs of children in those days."

He sighed and turned around, looked down at the street, his gaze lost in the past. "When I was about thirteen, I figured out that I wasn't human. At will, I could become invisible. It was my Sylph side coming out. I escaped the glassworks using that ability."

Of course. He was a half-breed. They didn't come into their powers until puberty, unlike full breeds, who developed them more gradually from the time they were infants.

"Then what?" she asked.

"I met Tommy. Fell in with his crowd of thieves, and have been doing it ever since. I left Tommy and his like behind years ago and struck out on my own. More profitable."

"You could do legitimate work," she said.

"What kind? I'm a former Mythean criminal. At least, I hope to be, if I can get out of prison." He fingered the collar at his neck and she wanted to yank the thing off him. There was no way he'd be getting out and it made her sick.

"Anyway," he said. "I enjoy the hunt. The chase. It's who I am."

Fiona's phone shrilled and jerked her attention away.

She looked down at the number. Fear clogged her throat, and it felt like the floor dropped away from her.

Her boss. Again.

The phone continued to shriek into the now-silent flat. Fiona knew her face was white, her eyes probably wide as hell.

Ian turned and walked to the couch, no doubt trying to give her a bit of privacy in the tiny flat. But she couldn't seem to pick up the phone. Her hand clenched around the little piece of plastic until the ringing finally stopped

A voicemail popped up and her stomach pitched. A second call from the boss who never called her. She was just a researcher and receptionist now. A desk jockey. There was only one reason he'd call her.

She took a shuddering breath and pressed the voicemail button, then lifted the phone to her ear.

"'Fiona, this is Darrence. Lea has informed me that you're searching for the book. You'll cease this ridiculous hunt immediately and return to the university at once. Retrieving the book is beyond your capabilities, as you've proven. The university will be sending in the best of the best tomorrow. Don't screw this up for them by charging in there and fucking this up. You'll be a disgrace to your family, as your father was. I want to see you in my office tomorrow morning, or we're sending guardians after you."

She dropped the phone into her lap. She'd known this would happen, she just hadn't thought it would be so soon.

Ian turned to her, concern darkening his expression. "Are you okay?"

"Fine. Gotta go." She raced to the bathroom. She swung the door shut behind her and leaned over the sink, her hands biting into the rim until her knuckles were as white as the porcelain.

She dragged frantic breaths into her lungs, struggling to calm her breathing and her pounding heart. *My job.* Everything she'd worked for. It had been a mess these last ten years, ever since she'd failed to find the book, but it was all she had. All she worked for. All she really wanted.

It was her life, as it had been her father's before her. Becoming a *Failte* had ruined it for her, but still, she needed this job. It was what she'd been fighting for, just as much as she'd been fighting to find the book to save herself from her father's fate.

Now they would try to take it from her?

Knocking sounded at the door.

"Just a minute." Fiona was horrified to hear the tears in her voice. She glanced up at the mirror and saw them streaking down her face.

Oh shite. She scrubbed at her face, but it only made her look redder and wilder.

Ian knocked on the bathroom door again. The muffled sounds of her tears echoed through the door.

"Fiona, let me in," he said.

"Just a minute."

Damn it, no. Just no. He couldn't stand on this side while she was distraught on that side. For the last hundred years, he'd been kept from what he wanted by prison walls. Now he wanted to comfort her, and he was separated by a damned bathroom door.

"I'm coming in." He twisted the doorknob. When the lock didn't catch and she didn't slam a hand against the door to stop it, he pushed it open and squeezed into the tiny bathroom behind her.

Fiona was leaning over the sink, her long hair pulled out of its knot and falling around her face. She stiffened when she sensed him behind her, then shook her head and turned to face him.

Her face was set, her eyes hard, and her lips firm. Suddenly he doubted whether or not she even needed him here to comfort her.

Then her lower lip trembled.

"Ah, Fiona." He opened his arms wide and pulled her into an embrace.

"I'm fine." Her words were muffled against his shoulder.

"Aye, 'course you are."

"I am." Her voice hitched.

"Come on, to the living room." He removed his arms and pushed her gently out of the bathroom. They sat on the couch. Unable to help himself, he wrapped an arm around her. She stiffened, then turned so that her back was pressed to his side and her face turned away from him.

She didn't remove his arm from where it wrapped around her shoulders and the top of her chest, though. She drew her knees up and her breath shuddered.

She scrubbed a hand over her cheeks and said, "Gods, I'm never like this."

"That, I believe," he said. From what he'd seen of her in the last twenty-four hours, he had a feeling this was the first time a tear had escaped her in decades.

"I haven't cried since my father was sent away to prison. There's no point in it," she said.

"Course there is. You feel better now, do you no'?"

"No' really."

"Well, it was bound to happen. This is a hell of a lot of stress for any one person. This is no' about just getting your old job back. You're trying to rewrite your fate and save yourself."

She turned to face him. "Aye. Exactly."

"You're more than just your fate, Fiona. Everything I admire about you has nothing to do with your fate. You're strong and determined and hard working. You have a noble purpose and goal. You work to save the past for others. I've never had that kind of goal. Just working to survive, to stay out of the poorhouse and now out of prison. Most people are like that. But no' you. You're so driven and skilled that you'll find the book, no matter what your fate says."

A great sigh shuddered out of her. "I'm such a weakling to be weeping about it, but I canna help it."

"What's so bad that it canna be fixed?" he asked.

"My department knows what I'm doing. They want me to come back or they'll send guardians after me. If I go back, I'll lose any chance at the book and I'll be a *Failte* forever. And they'll fire me, so I'll go mad all the sooner without work to distract me. But if they send guardians after me before we find the book, it'll be that much harder."

"When will they send them?"

"Tomorrow."

"Then we'll get the book tonight."

"We have to. Because it's more than just me. If I fail and the university fails to retrieve the book, we're looking at divine war before the end of the month."

"You'll get it back. I canna imagine another Mythean being more capable of the job. If you quit now, the university's best chance of getting the book back goes with you. Then we're all fucked."

She straightened and breathed deeply, her confidence and determination strapped back around her like a suit of armor. "You're right, damn it."

He grinned. He liked her toughness and determination.

We'll get this book," he said. But as he said it, dread settled in his stomach. The book was his ticket out. He had to have it to barter, or he had nothing and he'd be back in hell. But if he threatened to destroy it to force her to remove his collar, the university would fire her.

With the shaking nerves of her freak-out behind her, it suddenly hit Fiona that she was sitting pressed against the hard length of Ian's side.

The attraction she'd been suppressing welled, heat and warmth and grinding need rushing through her in a torrent. The stress of everything that lay in front of them broke down her resistance so that the river of want surged through her.

"Fiona?" Ian's voice scratched so sweetly over her nerves and made her sex throb. His voice was so rough and hard that she couldn't help but think he'd sensed the change in her.

"Aye?" Her voice was scratchy, too, she realized.

"Maybe you ought to get up."

She turned her head to look at him, but couldn't quite get the range of motion required. Instead, she caught sight of the bulge between his thighs, thick and long and so prominent that it was obscene.

She wanted it. She shouldn't. It was a terrible idea, a distraction from her work. But gods, she wanted it. Wanted him. Wanted something to make her forget everything that was at stake, if only for a moment. They had hours before they could break into the museum.

"It must have been a really long time since you've been with a woman."

Why had she said that? To egg him on? To explain to herself why he was hard for a boring Acquirer like herself?

"It's fine." His voice had turned to gravel and his breath feathered against her ear, making her shudder.

"Really?"

"I'm no' a fucking animal, even if I feel like one right now. But I'm at the edge here, Fiona, with the things I want to do with you. So I'm going to need you to get up or to tell me what you want." The arm that wrapped around her shoulders trembled, his self-control an iron thing bent to breaking. "Do you want this, Fiona?"

This was so crazy. It was happening so fast. But it'd been so long since she'd been with a man. And she wanted this man. He was handsome and charming and dangerous and a *thief.* Forbidden.

"Fiona?"

"Aye." It was so quiet she was almost afraid he didn't hear her.

But his big hands gripped her shoulders and spun her quickly, pressing her back into the seat, so that he could rise up hot and hard over her, caging her in.

His head dipped low and close, his eyes hot on hers. He smelled of clean soap and aroused male and it made her want to taste him. To run her tongue over the smooth skin that stretched across the hard muscles she knew covered all of him.

"You're sure?" Ian asked, his voice gravel.

The need and power in him almost overwhelmed her, but not so much that she couldn't nod.

Fierce pleasure streaked across his face and he pulled her to her feet. He cupped her head and pressed his mouth to hers, stealing her breath and making her head spin.

Her lips parted beneath his and she moaned when she felt his tongue against her own. Lightning bolts of sensation shot through her. He was too skilled for someone who hadn't kissed in nearly a century.

His big hands gripped her hips and plucked her off her feet. She wrapped her legs around his waist and gasped at the feel of his cock against her. One big hand gripped her arse, massaging.

"Gods, you feel so good. So *damn* good." His mouth pressed hotly to her neck. He inhaled deeply, taking her scent into him as he walked.

He stepped into the small, dim bedroom and headed for the bed. Gently, he lowered her to the mattress, then rose to stand tall.

She sat up and reached for him, brushing her hand against his arm. He trembled, a whole-body shudder.

The enormity of how long he'd been without touch, without sex, sent a rush of warmth to her pussy and made her want to spoil him. To kiss every inch of him and make him feel her hands, her lips, her tongue on every part of him.

He loomed above her, tall and hard and dangerous except for the fact that he would never, ever hurt her.

Oh, he was dangerous to her sanity.

She pulled back and looked up at him. "Just no' full sex. No' yet."

She was afraid she was falling for him already. She couldn't do that and walk away easily tomorrow morning.

"Aye. Anything. Anything you'll give me." His eyes raced over her face, full of wonder and desire and joy and every good thing she'd forgotten could be directed her way.

"Take your sweater off," she said.

He complied, ripping the wool over his head and tossing it on the floor. His arms dropped to his sides and her gaze traced over him, taking in the cut of his muscles and the veins that stood in sharp relief along his forearms.

He looked too perfect to be real, and the shadow at his jaw made her wonder what the scruff would feel like against her skin.

She reached for his belt, her fingers trembling at the contact with the cold metal buckle. She fumbled with it, wishing she were smoother. It finally came undone and she reached for his pants to draw down the zipper.

She looked up at him as she pulled, entranced by the heat in his eyes and the way his lips parted as he watched her.

The fabric parted, and with a push, dropped to the floor. Her gaze was dragged with it.

Oh.

He was beautiful. Thick and long and flushed, with lovely veins tracing delicate patterns along the sides. A pearl of fluid graced the tip, and her tongue itched to sweep it up. She wanted it. She wanted him. She wanted desperately to make this the best night he'd ever had.

She dragged her eyes up to meet his. "It's been so long for you. What do you want?"

CHAPTER SEVEN

Ian swallowed hard at the sight of Fiona, looking up at him, her pretty face so close to his cock that she could reach out and take him inside her mouth without straining her neck.

Fuck. He wanted everything. He wanted her lips wrapped around his cock, the heat of her mouth and the softness of her tongue. He wanted an orgasm that didn't come from his own hand. He wanted to touch her, to feel every inch of her body against his, sensory overload, as if he could banish all the lonely memories through touch alone. He wanted to bury his face in her pussy and lick her until she screamed.

But first he wanted to see her.

He pushed away the thoughts of stealing the book and said, "Take off your shirt." His voice scratched its way out his throat. He clenched fists that ached to rip the shirt off her.

She rose up on her knees and pulled the shirt over her head. Her pants followed. The breath rushed out of him. Soft white cotton cupped her breasts and her sex, leaving a long expanse of naked belly and thighs. He had no words for what she wore.

She was soft and curved and lovely. Everything he hadn't had in so damned long.

He reached out and cupped the back of her neck, his thumb sweeping over her cheek. "Lie down."

"Are you sure?" She reached out and grasped his cock in two soft hands.

"Oh, fuck." His hips jerked uncontrollably at the feel of her hands. Thoughts of spreading her out and licking and sucking and drowning in what he'd been missing fled his mind. He was nothing but the feel of her hands stroking his cock.

He felt like a gods damned wreck.

Her steel-gray eyes met his as she brought her lips to the head of his cock. Her pink tongue darted forth to stroke up the sensitive flesh. The sight was so hot his knees almost buckled.

"Gods, you doona have to." The words were torn from his throat—the truth, yet laced with desperate hope that she wouldn't listen.

Her answer was to envelop the head of his cock in the heat of her mouth. Unable to help himself, his eyes squeezed shut.

"I'm no' gonna last."

She sucked, made him jerk again, then drew away. "We'll see about that. Lie down."

He followed her down onto the bed, yanking the pants from his ankles and the socks from his feet. He let her push him onto his back. It'd been his plan to kiss her, stroke her, make her feel good. Show his appreciation for the gift she was giving him. He levered up on his elbows, tried to rise over her.

"Nay." She grasped the iron collar around his neck and pushed him to his back.

His collar. It was unbearably hot, and unbearably fucked up, to be maneuvered by the collar. He shouldn't like it, but fuck, he did.

"Let me take care of you," she whispered at his ear.

A shiver shot down to his cock and a ragged moan escaped his throat. He watched her kiss her way down his chest, desperately trying to memorize the feel of her lips and tongue on his skin.

She ran her hands up his chest and over his shoulders.

"You're so hot," she said against his stomach.

Vaguely, through the heat of her mouth and the buzz in his mind, he was aware of pride. He wanted to please her, was glad she liked the way he looked, so different from his past self. But mostly his mind was on her. On her mouth, on her breasts, which brushed his throbbing cock.

His arms shot up to the headboard when her mouth neared his cock. His hands bit in to the wood when he felt the brush of her breath against the throbbing shaft.

Teasing, not alighting.

"Please." The word broke from his throat as he looked down.

"Patience," she murmured, her eyes meeting his. "You're starving. This is like your first meal in a century. It could be fast and frantic or slow and decadent. Either way it'll be over and gone. Will it no' be better if it's savored?"

A groan escaped his throat and he dropped his head back onto the pillow.

Her hot breath returned to his heated flesh, shivering over him until he had to grip the headboard to keep from thrusting up toward her mouth. He felt her hand slide up his chest.

"Give me your hand," she said.

He let go of the headboard and reached for her. She took his hand and drew it to her head. Her soft hair tangled about his fingers.

"Show me what you like," she whispered, then returned to his cock.

Her lips closed around him, hot and wet and soft and perfect. But she stayed still, waiting for him. Gods, he'd never pushed a woman's head onto his cock before. Wanted to maybe, but it'd seemed damned rude.

Damn hot too, and knowing that she wanted it forced good manners and misgivings from his mind. His arm trembled as he pressed down lightly on her head. Watching his hand control her as she sank down onto his cock was insanely hot, made more so by the fact that she'd used his collar to control him just minutes ago.

She added her hand to the base of his shaft, a delicious friction that kept him from pushing too far. Together they found a rhythm, and soon his hips were rising off the bed, helplessly seeking her mouth.

Gods, she'd turned him into a fucking animal after all. Tension and heat and need coiled hard and fierce. He was so close—

She stopped. Withdrew her mouth and kissed his thighs.

"Fuck, I'm sorry, I should have told you I was close." Bastard. Of course she didn't want him coming in her mouth.

She bit his thigh and looked up at him. "I knew you were close. That's why I stopped. I'm no' done, though."

The heat of her mouth enveloped him once again. Hot and hard and fast, she sucked him. The orgasm rose more quickly this time.

"I'm close." His arms were shaking and his hips moving, helpless.

She drew her mouth away. He reached down to finish the job and she swatted his hand away.

"Mine."

"What?" he breathed.

"Slow and decadent, remember?"

Then her mouth was on his cock again, and all he could do was feel and moan and grip the headboard.

She stopped again and again, the graceless thrusting of his hips easily alerting her to when he was close. He thought he'd shatter every time she left him dangling on the precipice.

"Please." He couldn't help but beg. Every muscle in his body strained with tension from his desperation, his head spun, and his cock ached.

Her mouth returned, hot and wet, along with one hand on his shaft and the other cupping his balls. This time, when his body shook and his heels dug into the bed and his hips arched, she didn't let go. Her hot mouth licked and sucked and rubbed until he finally felt the orgasm coil within him, hot and harsh and fierce.

"I'm close. Gods, please." His body and mind strained toward that explosion. When her mouth didn't leave his cock, he cried out in gratitude. The orgasm roared through him, a force that pounded through his mind and body and cock until he felt it burst from him and into her mouth, jet after jet of the most incredible pleasure.

She stayed with him, taking what he gave and working his cock with hands and mouth until he was sure he'd come so hard he'd never come again.

When it was over, as his breath heaved in and out of his lungs and he stared blindly at the ceiling, he realized that her hands ran gently up his sides, soothing him as he shuddered and gasped. The tenderness made his chest ache. He felt exposed, raw, and part of his mind wanted to curl up and hide.

She kissed him once more, then crawled up his body to rest at his side. He used a trembling arm to drag her to him. The feel of her against him was a miraculous connection, the glory of which he'd forgotten about entirely.

His pride, his gratitude, made him want to turn the tables. Stretch her out and kiss every inch of her, fuck her pussy with his mouth until he turned her into the mess that he was.

But damned if he could even move right now.

"Thank you." His tone was embarrassingly reverent, but he couldn't fucking help it.

"I wanted to. I liked it."

"You're damned good at it."

"You were easy to read. All those gasps and moans and curses."

"Damn." He laughed, embarrassed.

"Nay, I liked it." She stroked his cheek.

"So did I. So much so that I canna even move. I'll need a few minutes, if it's all right, before I see to you."

"You doona need to do anything. It's no' something you need to pay back."

"The hell it is no'." He leaned down to kiss her, the effort sapping him even more. "And I want to. No' just out of gratitude, but desire. I have no' touched a woman in a century. Let me touch you. Let me make you feel good."

Let me be in control. He needed it now. As much as he'd needed the full body and mind fuck she'd given him with her mouth. He hadn't had a need for control in his first life, but after so long following someone else's orders in prison, and after losing his mind and body in Fiona, he wanted to be the one with the power.

She nodded.

"Good." He stroked her back, dozing in a twilight state, as he waited for his muscles to come back to life. It didn't take long. The scent of her arousal pulled him out of the twilight within minutes.

"Come here." He pulled her beneath him and grinned down at her. "Forgive me if I doona have your patience."

He pressed his lips hard to hers. She was hot and sweet and sexy as hell. Her body pressed full against his as he explored her mouth. He couldn't get enough of feeling her against him, warm and soft and *there*. There when there had been no one for years upon years.

Unable to wait any longer, he dragged his lips down her neck to her chest, licking and nipping along the way. He was going to kiss her everywhere, taste her everywhere. He was going to savor and spoil her.

She shifted beneath him, her thighs parting and her luscious scent drifting up to him.

Oh fuck.

He yanked her down the bed until her hips were at the edge and he was kneeling on the floor. He couldn't wait, had been crazy to think he could. He'd been so long without this. She might have made him go slowly before, but his control was shot.

He wanted to sink into her, to disappear in the wetness and softness at her core.

Fiona trembled when she felt his big hands grip her thighs. She leaned up on her elbows to see him kneeling at the foot of the bed, his eyes glued to her pussy. When he pushed her thighs wide apart, she gasped.

She was so exposed to his gaze it made her want to snap her thighs shut and hide.

"Beautiful," he breathed, then swept his big thumb up the length of her slit, parting her.

"Really?" She knew she should have played it cool, just accepted the praise, but damn, she couldn't help it.

His eyes met hers, hot with desire and need. "Aye. The sight of you, pink and wet, makes me hard as a damn rock."

"*Oh.*"

She watched, breath caught in her throat, as he draped her thighs over his shoulders and gripped her arse in two big hands. Suddenly, his mouth was on her, tongue seeking and stroking and making her arch into his mouth.

"Fuck, you taste good," he said against her flesh.

She could do nothing but whimper. He was ravenous, licking and sucking and making a glorious mess of her. Soon, she was arching off the bed, her spine curving uncontrollably to get her closer to his mouth.

"That's it, love," he muttered against her flesh.

"More." She gasped. She wanted more. She wanted him inside her.

"Aye, lass, I'll give you more." His fingers traced the edges of her sex, probing, exploring.

One thick finger slipped inside her and she jerked. His tongue was fast and frantic on her clit now, exactly what she needed, and when he pushed another finger inside of her, the need coiled tight inside her.

She dragged her head off the pillow, desperate for a glance of him working so hard between her thighs. The sight of his arm moving caught her eye. Was he touching himself?

The thought of his hand on his cock, turned on by what he was doing to her, pushed her over the edge. The orgasm tore through her, so hard that she felt her muscles clamp down on his fingers.

He groaned against her clit, his arm moving faster as he picked up speed on himself. The harsh noise that escaped him, as close to a growl as a man could make, threw her over the cliff again as he jerked and shuddered between her thighs.

CHAPTER EIGHT

Something heavy pinned her to the bed. Fiona's eyelids flew open. She lay on her side in the dim light of the small bedroom.

Ian's heavy arm clutched her to him, his head nestled in her hair. She could feel his breath on the back of her neck. They must have dozed off after he'd finished giving her so many orgasms she'd lost count. Her gaze jerked to the clock on the bedside table.

Only eight thirty. Her shoulders relaxed. So she'd only dozed for a few minutes, no doubt completely drained. Nerves over the coming night had been an excellent alarm clock.

Nerves that she'd somehow ignored to be with Ian. Memories of the last few hours flashed through her mind.

Holy crap. She'd had crazy sex with the prisoner she'd busted out of the university prison. The iron band around her wrist felt heavy, a physical reminder of her responsibility.

That she'd ignored.

But he wasn't just any prisoner; he was Ian. And she was naked in bed with him after the most incredible sex. She hadn't woken up like this with a man since before the book entered her life and she'd become obsessed with finding it.

Ever since she'd failed to find the book nine years ago, the time when the prophecy had specifically said she'd recover it, she'd started retreating from everyone around her. She'd been vaguely aware that she'd been doing it, but she'd told herself she was just focusing on work and fixing what she'd screwed up. It was more important than anything else.

Which was true. But looking back, she supposed that she'd been pushing people away. It was probably unhealthy, but she couldn't bring herself to care. It was how she operated best.

Until Ian. Until he'd somehow weaseled his way into her mind and maybe even a tiny corner of her heart. The idea terrified her and made her vaguely queasy. He'd be going back to prison, and now she was afraid she couldn't get enough of him.

No, it was just sex. Nothing serious. They barely knew each other. She'd just been in a drought. One she hadn't really noticed because of work, but a drought nonetheless. So had he. They were just helping each other out. And now she'd focus on work.

She nodded decisively, even though she knew it was a lie.

Ian made a sleepy noise and shifted. Quietly as she could, she crawled out from beneath his arm and crept out of the bedroom, intent on a shower. They still had at least an hour before they could break into the museum.

It didn't take much time to get cleaned up, but it was long enough that her mind started to zero in on her goals again, on the magnitude of the opportunity she'd been given.

By the time she made it back to the bedroom, Ian was sitting on the side of the bed.

"Hey." His voice was rough from sleep, his hair tousled.

Oh, he looked good. But she didn't know what else to say to this man who'd quickly become much more than a one-night stand. "Hey."

"Thanks for that." His eyes were sincere, and she felt heat climb into her cheeks.

"Sure."

The towel wrapped around her didn't feel nearly big enough. She walked to her bag, which sat on the chair, and fished around for jeans and a shirt. The heat of his eyes burned into her back as she dropped the towel and tugged them on. It was unexpectedly intimate to change in front of him and a shiver went down her spine.

"I'm going to shower."

She didn't turn to face him. "Okay. We've still got an hour before it's quiet enough to break in. I'm going to go keep an eye on the museum through the window."

"All right."

Her grip on her shirt loosened when she heard pipes squeal from the running water. A great sigh heaved out of her. Treating this as something casual wasn't going to be as easy as she'd hoped.

An hour later, Ian followed Fiona down the stairs and out onto the rain-dampened street. They'd spent the last hour at the window, surveying the museum to see if any of the god's demons would try to get in, but he hadn't been able to keep his mind off Fiona.

He couldn't help but feel like he'd been cleaned out. Like the worst of the fog that prison had cast over his mind had dissipated. It'd been a hell of an introduction back to the real world, but it had worked.

The whole time he'd been in prison, as new prisoners had told of the changes that were occurring in the outside world, he'd thought that the biggest thing he'd have to adjust to would be changing culture and technology.

He'd been wrong. It had been connecting with another person. He'd known he was lonely in prison, but he hadn't realized how much so until Fiona had shown up. The connection he felt with her reminded him that he wasn't broken after all.

She had done that for him. He felt pathetically grateful to her and helplessly intrigued. He'd wanted it to be just another shag. Like any of the nights with countless women before he'd been thrown in prison.

But it hadn't been. It'd been more. He liked her, more than ever now. Sure, maybe it was infatuation because she'd sprung him from jail. And she hated that he was a thief. Probably didn't even trust him.

But she'd been with him today, been more generous than he'd had any right to hope for, when he was at his lowest low. He wore a collar, for fuck's sake.

He glanced at her as she strode across the street toward the museum. Confidence blazed from her, brighter than the car headlights in the distance.

No woman had ever been with him when he hadn't been at his best. It had taken him nearly forty years to figure out the true extent of his powers and learn to use them well. Once Ian had accumulated some wealth, life had been fine. Women had flocked to him.

But when he'd been poor and powerless, no woman had ever wanted him. He couldn't blame them. Poverty had made him a mean bastard. Without charm or wealth, there'd been no woman willing to take a risk on him, especially not when they'd lived in a time when, more often than not, a woman needed a man to take care of her if she didn't want to face a life of poverty and never-ending drudgery.

But Fiona lived in the modern age. She took care of herself and had the freedom to choose anyone. Even a criminal. *Thank you, women's liberation.*

He shook his head. None of it mattered. As soon as they got to the book, he'd have to use it to force her to free him. She'd lose her job and hate him for it. Then he'd have to flee Scotland so that the university never found him again. There was no future for them.

Hell of a mess.

The blare of a car horn dragged his attention back to the present. They strode down the street in front of the museum, headed for the alley with the side door. Two figures stood at the alley.

"Shite," Fiona said.

Police. Right at the entrance to the alley, either guarding it because of last night or just running patrol on the popular street since it was a Friday night and the pubs were bursting.

"We'll have to go through the roof entrance," Fiona said, and walked past the police officers without a pause in her step.

He nodded. They turned at the next alley and made their way to the back of the museum. It was dark and silent in the back alley, with only dim moonlight illuminating the rain-slicked cobblestones. No pubs back here, so no people.

They reached the rear of the museum, a simpler construction of stone with few windows. A fire escape ladder crept up the side of the three-story building. Fiona walked to a tree in the middle of the small courtyard and broke off a dead branch. She broke it down until it was shaped like a hook.

"Can you give me a boost?" she asked when she returned to his side.

He nodded and lifted her, hoisting her over his head until she stood on his shoulders. For mortals, it would have been a feat of acrobatic strength. For Mytheans, it was nothing. Her legs were firm where he gripped her, trying to steady her as she reached up with her hooked branch and pulled the fire escape ladder down.

Metal screeched against metal. His shoulders tensed. Fiona hopped down and tossed her branch aside. They scaled the ladder quickly and hopped onto the roof. The small building with the door that led to the stairs was only ten yards away.

He was walking toward the end of his time with her, he realized. As soon as he had the book, he'd barter his freedom and be out of the there.

Shite.

CHAPTER NINE

Ian beat Fiona to the door and pushed it open to slip inside. She followed and eased the door shut. Quickly, she pulled a glass vial out of her pocket and unstoppered it. A pale blue mist wafted up from the top, a spell that would disengage the alarm.

Once she was confident that the police wouldn't be alerted, they crept down the stairs until they reached the door that led out into the exhibits. Ian pressed an ear to the wood to listen for the footsteps of the night guard. She drew the short sword she'd brought, having decided that since the odds of encountering the god's demons were so high, it'd be better than her daggers.

Eventually, he nodded at Fiona, palmed the dagger she'd given him, and slowly pushed open the door into the darkened room. The red exit light shone down from above, and dim white lights illuminated the long space that was cast in shades of gray. The room was full of ancient pottery. Enormous pots crouched on the floor while tiny vases decorated pedestals.

Ian motioned for her to wait in the doorway and stepped into the room. He walked to the nearest large pot and laid both hands on its round belly. When nothing happened, he turned around and nodded at her.

So that's how he deactivated the spells. They sensed him. She and Ian made their way through the pottery exhibit and stepped into the next room, a small one that contained eight tables displaying glass art and kaleidoscopes.

The darkness immediately turned to blinding color, geometric shapes spinning through the room in patterns made up of dozens of colors and designs.

"What the hell," Fiona whispered.

Pinks, purples, blues, and yellows in triangles and diamonds and pentagons shone from every inch of the room. She could no longer locate the artifact displays. They were in a giant kaleidoscope.

Fiona reached out and grasped Ian's hand. He pulled her until she stood behind him, her chest pressed to his back.

"Follow me exactly," he said.

Colored lights and shapes flashed before her eyes as she followed Ian. His steps were deliberate, and before long she realized they followed a specific pattern. She tried to put her feet where he'd put his, but suddenly she was stepping on what felt like pebbles. Shards of glass crunched beneath her soles. A second later, she was knee deep in pebbles and glass. The insides of the kaleidoscope were filling up the room.

"Ian!" she hissed.

"This is new. Hurry!"

They pushed their way through the bits of glass, slowing as it reached their chests. Shards cut her exposed hands, burning and turning her grip on her sword slick with blood. It was nearly to her neck. She could drown in this, sucking shards of glass into her lungs.

The glass bits were nearly to their mouths by the time they stumbled into the next room. Panting, she spun to look at the kaleidoscope room. It had returned to normal.

"What the hell!" she said. "You stopped the magic in the pottery room, but no' this?"

Ian shook his head, his hands laced with tiny cuts that dripped blood. "I tried. There was a specific route to walk through the room. I stayed on it, but it didn't work. The magic has mutated."

"So that's really possible?" She hadn't wanted to believe it. She peered at the tiny cuts on her hands. They were so small that they were healing quickly, thank gods.

"With this much time? Aye. Magic is no' my strength. We'll still get to the vault, it will just be trickier."

Shite. What about the rest of the museum? She looked around at the landing they'd stumbled onto. Wide marble stairs went three stories down to the main floor, with expansive marble landings on each level. In the middle of the stairwell, with the square-oriented stairs wrapping around it, was a huge steam engine from the late eighteenth century.

Boulton and Watt steam engine, the sign said, invented by the Scotsman James Watt. It was nearly thirty feet tall and thirty feet long. Its great wheel, beam, cylinder, and many pipes all looked gray and ominous in the low light of the stairwell.

"Wait here," Ian said.

She nodded and watched him sprint across the landing to the rail surrounding the stairwell. He leaned over and pressed his palm to the side of the steam engine.

The great beam and wheel of the engine creaked, then began to spin and pump.

Oh, damn.

It was turning on, steam pouring out of the machine magically fast and beginning to fill the space. Her skin burned from the heat.

"Shite," Ian said. "Come on!"

She ran to him. He grabbed her hand and yanked her down the stairs.

She could barely see, and stumbled at the first landing. Ian righted her.

Faster. If they didn't make it out of this stairwell soon, they'd burn to death in the steam filling the space. By the next landing, the metal hand rail had turned hot as a stove. She yanked her hand away and flew down the last set of stairs blindly, unable to see through the steam.

Her skin felt like it was on fire and her lungs were drowning in hot steam as she stumbled out of the huge stairwell and into the main lobby of the museum.

Sudden silence and cold. Her wet clothes stuck to her rapidly cooling skin as she gratefully sucked in the fresh air of the lobby. Ian stood next to her, panting and wet.

She nodded, still unable to speak, and propped her hands on her knees. When she'd finally caught her breath, she asked, "That was wrong too, wasn't it?"

"Aye. My touch should have deactivated the spell. But it dinna."

Damn. Stable magic was hard to create. So now, everything was going haywire. What would be coming at them next? They were still four rooms away from the basement entrance. The expansive lobby spread out from the stairs, the glass ceiling soaring three stories above. Moonlight shone upon the marble floor.

Fiona squinted toward the big admissions desk along the wall. It wasn't empty. A guard lay slumped over the desk, a dagger protruding from his back.

"Holy shite. The demons have beaten us here."

"Aye. Come on, then." Ian nodded toward the east wing. The entrance to the basement was tucked at the end, right past medieval, ancient, and geological history. If only it had been in the west wing, the one he'd blown up, the magic would all be gone. She could have sailed right though.

She cursed and followed him through the huge room, praying that the lack of artifacts in the lobby meant that there were no enchantments here to get them.

They hesitated at the entrance to the next room. Suits of armor. They lined the walls and marched down the middle of the room, metal gleaming dully in the dim light.

"These will fight us?" she asked.

"Aye. Give me a moment. And be ready to run." He slipped into the room and approached the first suit of armor along the wall. He set his hand on its shoulder and said, "I am Ian MacKenzie."

Fiona held her breath. The helmeted head nodded slowly, the metal shifting.

Ian's shoulders relaxed and he nodded at her. "Should be good."

She gripped her sword and followed him into the room. Her gaze darted around the space, watching warily for movement, but they made it through safely. They stopped at the entrance to the next room.

Weapons. Swords and daggers of all sizes lined the walls.

She waited and watched Ian step into the exhibit and press his back against the wall. She peeked around the entryway to see him inching toward a display of swords and shields. When he reached a great sword mounted on the wall, he gripped the hilt and paused. He scowled.

Damn, that couldn't be good. Ian left the sword and continued to inch his way down the wall toward the exhibit of shields. He yanked two off the wall, then moved back to her.

"Here. I doona think that worked." He thrust one into her arms. "Go fast."

Shite. She was immortal, but that didn't mean that beheading couldn't end her. She glanced at him, and bolstered by the steel in his gaze, turned back to the room. They set off at a sprint, the shields raised against the blades, and she'd have sworn that Ian held back to stay by her.

Swords and knives pried themselves off walls and shot through the air, pinging off the shields. She glanced around frantically, moving her shield to stop blades that hurtled from either side of the room. A dagger flew off the other wall and nailed Ian in the arm. Pain blossomed in her side and she reached for it. A slice across her abdomen wept blood.

Dozens of blades shot around the room. She dove left and narrowly avoided a sword headed straight at her. Ian flung himself right to avoid another blade, and soon they were separated.

As they limped over the barrier to the next room, she caught sight of the fallen, bloodied body of a demon that was just beginning to sublimate.

"Are you okay?" Ian asked when they stood in the threshold. His shield had half a dozen blades sticking out of it. Hers had more. The flying blades behind them clattered to the floor. A second later, the weapons returned to their original places on the wall and in display cabinets.

She peered down at her stomach and pulled the blood-and-water-soaked fabric away from her skin. The gash stung like a bitch, but it wasn't fatal.

"Fine. You?" She frowned at his arm, which was now liberally covered in blood.

"Perfect. That demon's corpse is no' more than a few minutes old," he said.

She nodded. Soon it would sublimate entirely and the soul would return to its afterworld. "We need to hurry."

Ian paused beneath the arch to the next room and peered in, tensed and wary. They'd made it safely through the last room—stone weapons that could pack a hell of a punch—but this endeavor had gone to shite. His enchantments had gone mad in the ninety-odd years he'd been in prison. Like a forest left to grow wild, the magic had grown and mutated. It should have been a stroll through the museum. But not with the changes. And they were far worse than he'd expected.

They hovered at the entrance of the Hall of Geology. Huge boulders lay like sleeping giants in the middle of the floor and smaller precious stones dotted the walls, pinned in their glass cases like flies. In the middle stood a statue of James Hutton, a Scotsman and the father of modern geology.

The door to the basement was at the other end of the room.

Ian looked at Fiona and nodded.

"Who are you and what is your purpose?" The statue bellowed.

The marble statue of James Hutton had awoken. Gleaming white hands were moving idly, swaying slightly, back and forth, the movement unnatural and eerie.

"I'm Ian MacKenzie," Ian said, and hoped for the best. James Hutton should let him through and fight all others.

"You are not he!" The statue's roar echoed through the huge room.

Shite. Of fucking course.

The great boulders crouched in the hall were moving as well, rolling back and forth as if they were trying to drum up momentum. They moved in sync with the statue's hands. Dread carved a black pit in his stomach.

The statue waved its marble arm, a fluidity to the motion that belied its substance.

A crack sounded and one of the huge boulders flew across the room, not rolling so much as hurtling through the air. Straight at them. Ian and Fiona dove away from each other, out of range of the boulder. The air whooshed as the boulder shot behind him. It crashed against the wall and fell still.

Lungs bellowing, Ian surged to his feet as Fiona did the same. Another crack of sound and a great column of marble flew at them from the opposite side of the room. He dodged it by a foot, Fiona by less.

"Run for the vault," Ian yelled. He had no fucking clue what was going on.

Speed was the only thing that could get them out of here. They had no way to fight the sheer power of the rocks. If just one caught them, they'd be crushed to death.

Fiona scrambled to her feet and took off toward the far exit. He followed just behind. Halfway through the room, they had to dive to the floor as the precious stones flew out of their glass cases on the wall and hurtled toward them like bullets—rubies, diamonds, emeralds glinting in the low light.

Several lodged themselves in his right arm and leg. He looked up through the arm that shielded his face and saw Fiona flinch as some of the stones hit her.

An unfamiliar protectiveness welled within him, tightening his throat and making his fists clench. So unfamiliar, but so strong. He crawled to her and threw himself over her. She tensed, then stilled. Finally, the sting of stones stopped.

"Go," he said.

She scrambled to her feet and he followed, taking off with only twenty yards between them and the entrance to the basement. From behind, the sound of creaking and groaning echoed through the room. Like a great iron bridge breaking. He swore he could feel the reverberations through his chest.

Ian glanced left. A hulking boulder, like the stone trolls of myths, hurtled across the floor, headed for Fiona.

It was a split-second decision, all instinct and no thought. He surged for Fiona, knowing that the boulder would likely crush him as he pushed her out of its way. His instincts had moved him and his body had followed. His brain had no say in it.

A thousand pounds of stone slammed into his back. The crash of their collision sent a bolt of agony from his shoulders to his feet.

He collapsed on the floor, his body a crushed mess of pain. Thank gods the boulder wasn't on top of him. It had bludgeoned him in the back and hurtled into the wall. The rest of the stones had fallen still. The spell was done, but this could have killed him, for gods' sake. What the hell had he been thinking?

"Nay!" Fiona's scream echoed in his head. "Ian!"

She'd been what he'd been thinking, he realized. Shite. That was unexpected.

She knelt over him and prodded at his back. He groaned at the stab of pain.

"Where does it hurt?" she asked.

Everywhere. He closed his eyes and sucked in a steadying breath. The agony that had streaked through his back was fading now, courtesy of Mytheans' speedy healing ability.

He gritted his teeth and pushed himself to his knees. There were definitely some broken bones. A few ribs, maybe his scapula. But even that was fading. It'd take some time to heal, but he could function.

"What the hell were you doing?" Fiona cried.

He hesitated. The truth of what he'd done, what it meant about his feelings, stared him in the face. Admit to her that he'd been willing to die for her? Hell, he didn't know how to process that. How would she? It was crazy.

Her eyes turned stark, dark in her pale face. "You sacrificed yourself for me. That was..." She looked around the room as if she'd find the word she wanted lying in the corner. "That was so stupid."

"What?" That was not what he'd expected.

Or was it? She was right. It'd been stupid. Ever since he'd walked out of the slums of Old Town as a boy, he'd dragged himself from misery by looking out only for himself. Caring for someone, like the old woman who'd brought him up before he'd gone to the workhouse, ended with abandonment. Willingly or not, people left you.

Helping, giving to others got you nowhere. Looking out only for himself had gotten him through life, turned his dirt-brown past into something brighter.

Then he'd met her, and so quickly, so blindingly quickly that it had happened almost without him realizing it, he'd sacrificed himself for her. In all his life, he'd never even considered sacrificing himself for someone else. Not even Logan.

But with her, he hadn't had time to think. Instinct had taken over. His subconscious seemed to know more about what she meant to him than his mind did. He had no fucking clue how to deal with that.

"It's done. Forget it." He knew the words were harsh, the tone worse. But he didn't know how else to be.

"I doona see how that's possible."

"It does no' matter," he gritted. "The demons are still ahead of us."

"Gods, you're right. But this is no' finished." Her eyes were flint hard.

He staggered to his feet. She raced ahead to the basement door. Ian limped to keep up. He'd better start healing faster. They hadn't a second to lose. If the demons were a species that could aetherwalk, they'd be back in their afterworld seconds after finding the book.

The basement door was cracked open just slightly, the lock no longer engaged. Ian palmed his knife. They passed through the door and crept down the white linoleum stairs, the tension in the air thick as custard. A long white hall stretched before them. Doors on either side led to offices and laboratories, according to the their plaques.

At the end, a door as unassuming as the rest led to the vault. There'd be a sturdy, locked door beyond it that really kept people out.

Ian took one last look at Fiona. They locked gazes for the briefest of seconds, then headed toward the demons.

CHAPTER TEN

Fiona crept down the hall behind Ian, her eyes on his broad back and the door in front of him. His limp had lessened. Some Mytheans healed more quickly than others, and he was in his prime.

Her heart pounded against her ribs, a desperate tattoo. They reached the end of the hall. The first door, the one without locks, was cracked open as the door at the top of the stairs had been. Fiona peered through the lower part of the crack and felt Ian do the same above her.

The space between the false door and the heavier one was small, not more than five feet, and beyond it the heavy vault door was swung open to reveal a large room full of shelves and bins and drawers.

"Not here," a gruff voice said from within.

Her eyes tracked the voice to the far corner, behind a shelf. She couldn't see enough to identify the species.

"Nor here," another voice answered. This one higher pitched, possibly female. Fiona couldn't see her either, but it sounded like she was closer and on the left side of the room.

"Gelve? Rone? Any luck on your side?" The gruff voice from the back asked.

They would say no, Fiona knew. She could sense the book like she had sonar in her mind. It was tucked all the way back in the very farthest left corner of the room, possibly even in a secret drawer.

A *no* and a grunt were the only answers. Fiona waited to see if any more would speak. Four against the two of them.

Fiona looked up at Ian.

"Four," she mouthed.

He nodded once, his expression grave.

She held up one finger, then pointed to herself and mouthed, "I can take one."

She was a good fighter, but combat wasn't in her job description. Saying she could handle more would just get them screwed.

Ian looked at her hard, as if trying to decide if she really could. She scowled back. She had a damn good chance at taking one of the demons, especially the smaller one with the high voice. At least, she assumed it was smaller.

Finally, Ian nodded. He pointed to himself and mouthed, "Three."

Her brows rose. *Three?* Really? Many species of demons could be as big and as dangerous as the Mythean Guardians. So far, she'd only ever seen the clever thief side of Ian. But if he said he could fight, she believed him.

He leaned in and pressed his mouth to her ear. "Take off my collar so that I can go in first, invisible, and see where they are. I'll go to the back wall. When I reappear, go for your demon."

Shite. He wanted her to take off his collar? He could run off on her. But he'd just risked his life for hers. He wouldn't ditch her. Right? She bit her lip. She had no idea.

But he was right—it would help their chances if he could fight while invisible.

"Fine. But it goes back on immediately after."

"Harsh." But he grinned.

She nodded and pulled it off.

Without warning, he disappeared.

Wow. She'd never seen his Sylph powers before, but now she understood why he'd been such a damn good thief. The descendants of air spirits really had an advantage. She trained her eyes on the back wall of the vault and waited for him. A little part of her itched with the idea that he was headed back up the stairs toward freedom, but a bigger, more insane part of herself trusted him.

Ten seconds later, he flashed visible at the back of the vault and disappeared again. As quietly as she could, she rushed into the vault, shot to the left, and came upon her prey.

It faced away from her, but damn, was it tall. Very slender, though, and of indiscernible species.

Less than a second later, the sound of a groan and a thud came from the back of the room. Ian had taken care of the first.

Fiona raised her sword and swung it at the demon, who spun just in time and took the barest nick from her blade. It faced her, revealing the eerie features of some type of Caoineag half-breed. Not a demon, then. Caoineag, as Highland banshees were called, were fierce and deadly. A full-breed Caoineag would still be in the forests, but this one wouldn't be limited by that and would have all the powers of her banshee brethren.

The Caoineag shrieked, a wail so high and sharp that Fiona's ears felt like they'd exploded. The pain nearly sent her to her knees, but she stiffened and raised her sword again. She struck and missed.

The Caoineag yanked her own sword from the scabbard at her side, flipping long black hair away from her face. The banshee's sword clashed against her own with a ring of metal. Pain sang up Fiona's arm from the collision, and she fought back, striking hard.

Fiona landed a blow to the banshee's arm. The banshee shrieked, but held onto her sword and swiped it across the front of Fiona's hip.

She gasped. Though shallow, the wound burned like acid. *Shite.*

As Fiona stumbled backward, she caught sight of another demon out of the corner of her eye. He was an enormous, hulking beast. A demon of some kind, no doubt, and his huge head swung as he glanced around frantically, looking for the threat that had killed his partner.

Then his head toppled from his body.

Ian. She couldn't see him, but gods, was he strong, to take such a big demon's head straight from its body. He would have had to leap into the air when he struck.

Fiona returned her attention to the Caoineag. With a burst of strength, she took advantage of an opening and plunged her sword into her opponent's gut. The banshee shrieked and fell to her knees. The piercing cry made Fiona crash to her knees as well, her head ringing.

She pried her eyes open, searching frantically for the other enemies. Her gaze raced around the room until it fell upon a pale, slender individual whose skin was traced with geometric black tattoos.

He was standing right in front of the drawer that held the book.

Nay. She stumbled to her feet as Ian surged toward the demon. In his haste, he seemed to have lost his invisibility. One of them just had to reach the demon in time. Before he—

The demon reached into the drawer, then disappeared. The book went with him.

"Nay!" Fiona collapsed to her knees again. "Nay!"

"Fuck!" Ian yelled.

"He's— he's—" *Gone.* She couldn't wrap her mind around it. He'd grabbed the book and aetherwalked to safety.

It was gone. A sob tore from her throat. Her fists clenched painfully around nothing. Her future was gone. But worse, the tool that could incite divine war was about to be in the hands of the rogue god who wouldn't hesitate to use it.

"Shite, Fiona. What are we going to do?" Ian's rough voice pulled her back from the edge.

She drew in a ragged breath. She had to get it together. "You're partners with Logan. I know it. Contact him. Ask for his connection, the Mythean who bartered his deal with the god."

Ian said nothing.

"Doona screw with me, Ian. There's no way Logan knew to bring you in here unless you were friends."

"Fine. We were. But he's gone. I've no way to get in touch with him."

The severity of his voice convinced her. *Damn it.* She tried to shove her panic aside as her mind scrambled for options. "I'm calling Lea. She might recognize his description. We have to know what afterworld he went to."

"Gods, it could be any of them. There's no way to know if he's native to the afterworld he just went to."

Her heart thudded sickeningly. Ian was right. But it was their only shot. She yanked her cell out of her pocket and dialed Lea. Her words tumbled over themselves as she described the demon.

"Damn," Lea said. "You went in alone."

"Of course I did. What did you expect?"

Lea sighed. "That you would. And thank gods for it. The university has just gotten together a team to send out in an hour, but they'd have been too late. I'm going to have to do some research to identify that demon."

"We doona have that kind of time."

"I know! But we don't have a choice, because I don't recognize the demon you're talking about. I'm going to get everyone on it. And we have to find someone who can get us to whatever afterworld it was taken to."

Shite. She was right. Certain Mytheans could aetherwalk, but not many of them had free access to all the afterworlds. Very, very few did. It'd take time to find someone who could get them there. Too much time.

"We're coming there," Fiona said.

"Good. It won't take long to get the word out. The council will be together by the time you get here."

The council. The ones who'd demoted her and stripped her of her position when she'd failed to find the book. Her shoulders tensed.

Fuck it. It didn't matter, not in the face of all this.

She mashed the *End* button and struggled to her feet. "We've got to get to the university."

"Aye."

They were able to exit via the alley door on the first floor, allowing them to avoid the charmed exhibits. Fiona didn't know if she could face them in her condition, and Ian was still limping. Thank gods the police were gone from the alley. The dark concealed their bloodstained clothes as they crossed the street toward the flat.

It took only minutes to retrieve the car keys and their possessions. There'd be no reason to come back here. Once they'd replaced their blood-splattered clothes with clean ones, she approached Ian with the collar and snapped it about his neck before he could stop her.

"Really?" he asked.

She nodded, her chest feeling tight. "The council will need to see that you're wearing it."

He frowned, but beneath the annoyance she swore—hoped—she saw understanding.

"How's your arm?" she asked as they descended the stairs to street level.

"Healing."

She nodded. He'd torn up a shirt and tied it around his arm. If it was still a problem when they got to the university, they'd have a healer look at it. She wouldn't mind having her hip and stomach gashes looked at. The wounds wouldn't kill her, but a bandage would be nice.

They slipped into her hatchback and took off through Edinburgh. It was after midnight and the streets had quieted.

Fiona was vibrating with tension by the time they drove through the university gates. She'd hoped to return through these gates with the book in hand, fate proven, sanity saved, and her old job won back. She was returning a failure. A true *Failte*.

Her lips tightened. Not for long.

She parked her car beneath the same tree she'd put it under when she'd sprung Ian from prison. She climbed out and looked over the roof at him.

"I'll see to it they doona put you back in that cell," she said. They'd be going back into the Praesidium, the same building that housed the prison in the basement. Lea's office happened to be in on the first floor.

He nodded, his lips tight and his eyes doubtful. Her heart sank, because though she'd fight to keep him out, her power didn't extend that far. But they didn't have a choice about going into the Praesidium. They had to get the book back.

They crossed the cobblestone lot and climbed the expansive stairs to the looming stone building. A chill raced over her skin as they walked into the atrium. The glass ceiling soared above the gleaming wooden floor.

"Doona worry about Lea," Fiona said as they walked down the hall. "She's going to look like a ghost, but she's no'. And she's harmless."

"What is she?"

"I doona know. She's just fading. It might have something to do with the fact that she never leaves her office. It's a library that she had expanded into a suite, but she hasn't left in at least a hundred years. Maybe longer. She's the best at what she does, though. She knows everything there is about

Mythean history, or where to find it. And she's one of the top ranking officials."

"Good thing she's on our side," he said when they reached a wooden door.

"Exactly." Fiona knocked.

CHAPTER ELEVEN

Ian followed Fiona into the library office.

"Fiona, that was quick," said a pretty, but transparent, woman. She turned to him. "You must be Ian."

"I am." He didn't offer his hand for fear of offending her if she couldn't take it.

She gestured to a table surrounded by a dozen chairs. All were occupied, though he recognized no one. Towering bookshelves loomed behind them. He and Fiona took seats next to each other. Her expression had turned to stone.

At the end of the table sat a disgruntled-looking man who glared at Fiona. Fiona's boss, no doubt.

Lea sat. "We're here to discuss the matter of the Book of Worlds."

"Damn straight we are," said the man who Ian had assumed to be Fiona's boss. "You were out of line, Fiona! You're no longer an Acquirer, and you had no business being in that museum."

"Without her, you'd have no idea who took the book," Ian said.

Fiona shot him a look that said *thank you, but be quiet.*

"He's right, Darrence," Fiona said. "It's my fate to find it. I *have* to find it. I'm the only lead we have on the book, and I'm sure as hell going to retrieve it."

"You're in trouble. And as for you, Ian MacKenzie. Don't think I don't recognize you. You're going to be back in that cell before you can blink. You're a—"

"Enough." Lea shot Darrence a quelling look. "We have more important problems. Rest assured, the prisoner will be sent back. But we must address the issue of the rogue god."

Ian's stomach lurched at the mention of being sent back to that hellhole. There was no way he'd let that happen. Fiona caught his eye and frowned. Darrence grunted but quieted, his look promising retribution.

"Did you identify which afterworld the demon went to?" Fiona asked.

"I did." A blond woman leaned forward. She sat at one head of the table, across from Lea. Her skin emitted a faint glow. "I'm Aerten, Celtic goddess of fate and leader of the Praesidium. And from the description you gave of the demon's tattoos, I think I know who stole the book. His tattoos indicate that he's a minion of Carthe, a god from one of the pantheons that started the Divine War that led to the creation of the covenant thousands of years ago. You recall the stories of the war?"

There were a few murmurs of assent and Ian nodded along with everyone else. He'd never learned the stories as a child like other Mytheans, but he'd been told about them in prison. The war had occurred thousands of years ago in Eastern Europe, at a time when the Roman gods were busy in Italy and the Celtic gods in Britain. But the continent had been a mess. Four groups of gods from four different pantheons—all lost to mortal memory now because they'd destroyed themselves—had erupted into war on earth. The gods had come down to the mortals in an attempt to gain more worshipers. Not unlike the visits that the Roman gods had paid the Romans.

But there'd been too many gods. Too many choices on display for the mortals. It had erupted into war. The mortals fought for their one true religion, and the gods fought to be the leaders of it.

They'd nearly wiped out the entirety of the four pantheons and the mortals who fought the wars, until finally, with few left to worship and even fewer to rule, they'd convened to discuss the future. To save their own hides and ensure that nothing like that happened again, they'd agreed to sign the covenant that would allow gods to visit earth, but only in limited numbers and not for the purposes of war or gaining more worshipers. Other gods who hadn't been involved in the war had agreed after seeing what had become of the pantheons that had engaged in war on the continent.

"So, Carthe dinna like the restrictions of the covenant?" Fiona asked. She caught Ian's gaze, then looked away.

"Not at all," Aerten said. "He was one of the dissenters to the original covenant. He was forced to sign anyway, of course, and agree not to come to earth to seek more followers, and thus more power."

"So why start something now? It's been thousands of years," Ian said.

Several murmurs from the council echoed his sentiment. Darrence glared at him, but he didn't bother to respond.

"As punishment for the Divine War, Carthe's afterworld and the others that started the fight were closed off. The sentence was just lifted a couple hundred years ago. That's probably when he started to look for the book," Lea said.

"Didn't anyone foresee that as being a problem?" Darrence asked.

"That they'd go for the book once their afterworld was reopened? Nay, because we never expected to lose it in the first place. We thought it'd be safe with us," Lea said.

Arrogance had never been in short supply at the university.

"So the book is in Carthe's afterworld. How do we get there?" Fiona asked.

"I can get you there," a dark-haired woman said. "But Dalen, as their afterworld is called, is hard to access. It will take me time to find the path through the aether."

"Vivienne is new to the world of myth," Lea said. "Barely a month ago she discovered that she's a Jinn of the Sila subspecies and that she has full access to the aether and all its afterworlds."

"But because I've never been there, it will take me some time to find the path," Vivienne said.

"How long?" Fiona asked.

"A few hours. A day."

"There's no way faster?" Lea asked.

"No. But we can leave as soon as I find it. I can take up to four people."

"Good," Fiona said. "Myself and Ian and two others."

"Don't think you're going after it!" Darrence said.

"The hell I'm no'," Fiona said. "We need a Historius to track it, and I know the signal. No' to mention that it's my fate!"

"She's right," Aerten said. "It *is* her fate. And she's already close to it."

"Then he's not going." Darrence pointed at Ian.

Gods, he was being a bastard just to be one. But several of the other council members were murmuring their agreement.

Fiona caught Ian's eye, then said, "He comes too. He's a Sylph. If we're going into an afterworld, we sure as hell canna kill the gods. They'll be too powerful. Our only chance is to sneak in and steal the book. We'll need his invisibility."

Darrence opened his mouth, but Lea cut him off. "It's done. Her logic is too sound to ignore. Fiona and Ian will go to Dalen with two Mythean Guardians. Ian's collar will be modified so that he can use his invisibility."

"Fine. But they'll be dragging him back to his cell as soon as it's done." Darrence's head looked like it might pop off his neck.

Bloody bastard. No doubt he was still angry about all the artifacts that Ian had stolen—or destroyed—over the course of his career. Acquirers hated treasure hunters more than most.

"I'll get to work seeking the afterworld. I'll let you know when I find it," Vivienne said.

"Thank you," Fiona said.

CHAPTER TWELVE

After having Ian's collar modified and stopping by the healer to have their wounds tended, Fiona and Ian rode to her house in silence. Thank gods they hadn't thrown him back into his cell for the night. They had faith in the collar, and she wondered if Lea had pulled a few strings. Though there was no reason to go back to the flat, part of Fiona wished desperately to be able to. To go back in time before she was certain Ian would be imprisoned again. Once she'd grown to like him, she'd hoped his service in helping retrieve the book would get him a reprieve.

How wrong she'd been. Everything with the book and the gods and her damned career was flying out of control, and her feelings for Ian were following suit.

Ian. Who had risked his life for her. Gods, she'd been in the archives so long that she'd forgotten this job could actually kill a person.

The pressure to find the book, to fix her fate and her life, had been building slowly over the last five years. It had taken her father a decade to go mad. She was getting close. Now, with all that was happening, it was like one of those great boulders in the Hall of Geology. Bearing down on her until she would be crushed.

She parked her car in the little drive and climbed out. Silence made her thoughts echo louder in her head as she let Ian into her house. She shut the door behind them and flipped on the light in her little living room. The dullness of her life blared at her. Boring white walls and books and reams of paper. Fluffy Black trotted out from the bedroom to greet her. Tufts of wild black fur stuck out of her at all angles, and bright green eyes peered up at Fiona demandingly.

As least she had Fluffy. She reached down and picked up the cat and hugged her, absorbing comfort from the small body. Ian walked up to stand before her.

"A cat?"

Fiona nodded, her mind drowning in worry. "Fluffy Black."

The corner of his mouth kicked up and he rubbed Fluffy's head. Fluffy's rumbly purr vibrated against Fiona's chest.

"No' the cleverest name. Yet you're a verra clever woman."

"No' when it comes to naming cats." What would happen to Fluffy if she never recovered the book? Fluffy squirmed, and Fiona realized that she was holding her too tightly. Fiona set Fluffy on the ground.

"Doona fret." Concern gleamed in his black eyes.

"I doona know how to stop."

He reached out and pulled her against him, his hands cupped around her neck and back. His lips were hot and soft on hers, devouring. Feeling hit her like a heat wave, and propelled by the madness of her life and her despair over the possible future, she kissed him back, throwing herself into it.

It was crazy. She'd known him such a short time but she didn't care. She wanted to forget it all for a while. She wanted him.

The low groan that tore from his throat spoke of desire and longing that had been building for decades.

She shuddered, the memory of him getting nearly crushed by the boulder too horrible to contemplate. It just made her more desperate, made her kiss him back so hard that her mouth would surely bruise.

What a terrible pair they made—an unrepentant convict and an Acquirer—yet she found it hard to care about that when his tongue thrust into her mouth and stroked.

His arm, roped thickly with muscle, wrapped around her waist, and he pulled her against his chest. She raised trembling hands and ran them over the cut pecs and abs she'd admired the other night.

Aye, it was very hard indeed to think of why this was a bad idea.

"More," she whispered, and gasped when he swept her up into his arms. "The bedroom is down the hall."

His footfalls were no longer thief-light as he strode toward the bedroom and it thrilled her to know his control was fraying.

He laid her on the bed and tore off his shirt before following her down. The hall light glinted off the hard lines of his muscles and made her fingertips itch to touch him.

She swallowed and raised her arms to him. He put a knee on the bed, then crawled up between her thighs and settled himself between them, his face level with hers.

The heat and hardness of him made her gasp.

"I want you, Fiona, more than I've ever wanted anything."

She pulled his head down to her, kissing him until her head spun and her breath heaved in and out of her chest.

"Gods, you feel good." He pulled his mouth from hers and traced his way down her neck.

She reached down to his fly, the zipper cutting into her fingertips. She barely got her fingers inside, barely brushed the heat and hardness of him, before he lifted her arms away and pinned them over her head.

"Careful, lassie, or this will no' last as long as we'd hoped."

"I doona care." She pulled against his arms.

He let go, but before she could reach for him again, he'd shifted down the bed and out of her reach. She dropped her head back on the pillow and gripped his shoulders. Cold air kissed her stomach as he pushed her shirt up, followed by the heat of his mouth. She arched beneath him when his lips traced her ribs.

Desperate, she yanked the shirt off. He quickly unclasped her bra and kissed her nipples, tracing the sensitive skin with his tongue until she was panting.

"I wanted to savor you." His words formed a delightful pattern against her nipple. "But I find that it's still too difficult to go slowly."

He swiftly unbuttoned her jeans and yanked them from her hips, taking her underwear with them. She felt his hands tremble as he parted her thighs, heard the groan that tore from his throat.

She jerked when he pressed his mouth, hot and open, to her sex, and plunged his tongue deep. He stroked and licked and sucked until her head was thrashing back and forth on the pillow and the room dimmed out of her vision.

The taste of Fiona made Ian's mind fog and his cock hard enough to drive nails. The way she arched off the bed, pressing herself to him, made his control flag. He'd wanted to take this slow, to savor her and the things they did together.

His body had different ideas. Tension and lust tightened his muscles and his mind and made him into the animal he'd so often protested he wasn't.

Fiona cried out and her body started to jerk against him, her orgasm making her twist on the bed.

Need suddenly crashed over him, dark and strong. The desire to be inside her, to feel her clutch around his cock, grabbed hold of him. He drew his mouth away and surged up over her body until they were face to face.

"So beautiful," he whispered. Her skin was flushed and her eyes bright.

"I need you inside me."

The words made him shudder.

She drew his head down to hers and kissed him hard, then arched her hips against him until the wetness of her core pressed against his cock.

He lost control of the kiss and groaned against her lips, the sound as close to that of an animal as a man could make. She was hot and wet and soft and so fucking perfect.

He lifted his head from hers as he fisted his cock and placed it at her entrance. The heat and wetness of her kissed the head of his shaft, making him want to drive home hard and fast.

"Now." Her voice was needy, and it made his chest swell. *She wanted him.*

He pushed into her heat, catching her gaze as he did so. He tried to watch her, to hold her gaze as her body enveloped him, but the blinding pleasure forced his eyes closed as it gripped him in a whirlwind.

So much fucking better than he remembered.

"More," she said.

Ian's body took over and he surged inside of her. He shuddered, dropped his forehead to hers, then picked up a rhythm that had her gasping and clutching at his shoulders.

The way her pussy gripped his cock made his balls tighten and his mind blur until he was just a mass of feeling. He wanted to hold back until she came, but his body was tightening up and the orgasm was rising relentlessly.

In a burst of energy, she shuddered beneath him, her core spasming as an orgasm wracked her. Immediately, his hips lost their rhythm, thrusting gracelessly as his body took over and sought that crashing wave of release.

When it hit him, hard and fast, his head jerked back and a roar tore from his throat. The gripping, enormous power of the thing made him shudder and heave over her, completely lost in his mind and his body and out of control.

Finally, it passed. He opened his eyes to look down at her, utmost contentment fighting with nerves. He'd lost his mind temporarily. Had he hurt her?

No. From the hazy smile on her face and the softness in her eyes, no.

He rolled off of her and dragged her to him, pulling her against his side. It had all happened so fast and —

Oh shite. His eyes popped open.

"I dinna use protection," he said. As Mytheans, they couldn't pass disease. But pregnancy, that was a problem.

Though would it be so bad?

"I'm fine," she said, her lazy voice interrupting the insanity of his thoughts. "I have an IUD. It's a little device that prevents pregnancy. That was amazing, by the way."

His head dropped back on the pillow, relief and disappointment surging through him.

Oh, fuck. He really was losing it. To even contemplate her being pregnant with joy? He could still be sent back to prison, for gods' sakes.

Yet the idea held undeniable appeal. Sacrificing himself for her back at the museum had been crazy, as she'd said. But it had also felt natural. And good.

But it didn't matter how he felt about her. Prison awaited him at the end of this if he didn't steal the book from her and force her to release him. Losing her job would crush her. He'd seen how important it was to her. And she'd hate him for it.

Hell. Falling for her was only creating more impossible problems. And he already had enough of those.

CHAPTER THIRTEEN

"Okay, we'll be there soon." Fiona hung up with Lea and glanced at the clock. Four thirty in the morning. They'd only gotten a few hours' sleep, but it was for the best.

"Vivienne has found the way to Dalen?" Ian asked. He looked so good, stretched out on her bed.

"Aye. We can go over there now."

He nodded and then climbed out of bed. Her muscles ached from exhaustion and use, but her mind was raring to go. As she dressed, her thoughts whirled in circles. She couldn't banish the memory of what had just happened between them, or her fear of the future.

She was falling for him.

Which was crazy. It had been such a short time. Her life was in shambles. How could this be happening to her?

But she couldn't help it. Gods, she was an idiot.

And they were screwed. Ian was going to be thrown back in prison. Last night, the university council members had been clear on that. They had the power to ensure it.

The university played with them like puppets. And it pissed her off.

She shoved on her shoes and went to the closet. She rifled through the clothes, squinting into the dark. Near the back she found an old turtleneck sweater. She pulled the black wool out and eyed it.

It should be big enough. Her brother had left it here ages ago, but he was nearly as big as Ian.

"What's that?"

Fiona turned to see Ian, dressed and ready to go.

She held out the sweater. "This is for you."

"Thanks." Confusion edged his voice. "You doona like my clothes? I doona blame you. They're glorified prison attire."

"That's no' it. None cover your neck."

Surprise flashed across his features and he raised his hand to his neck.

Bracing herself to break a damn big rule and possibly throw this whole thing in the toilet, she thrust the sweater into his hands. "Wear the sweater so that no one else knows the collar is gone."

His eyes flashed to hers, shock in their bright depths. "You'd really take it off?"

"If you promise no' to run until we find the book. I need your help."

"You could lose your job if you let me escape. That's what you've worked so hard for all these years."

The idea carved out a hollow place in her chest, but she realized that it wasn't nearly as big as the hole that would be left if he had to go back to prison.

"The most important thing is saving my sanity. Let me worry about my job. I thought I wanted it more than anything except my sanity, but if they're all going to be such assholes, maybe I was wrong." She raised her hands to his neck, snapped the collar in half, and drew it away. "When this is over, you'll run for it. If you stay in Scotland, they'll find you. You can never come back." The idea of never seeing him again plunged an icicle through her chest.

She turned from him, intent on heading to the bathroom. She couldn't look at him now, not knowing whether this was going to be over before it started. At best, he'd leave Scotland and never return. At worst, he'd be thrown back in prison. Or get killed.

"Wait." His hand closed around her arm and he spun her around. "It's no'—"

She threw herself into his arms and kissed him, the stress and fear of what she would lose propelling her to take one last grasp at it before it was all over.

He dropped the sweater, a groan rumbling out of his chest as he kissed her back. His mouth was hot and hard on hers, his hands everywhere.

She tore her mouth from his. "We need to go."

"When this is all over, I'm running. I'll be at the Keane Hotel in Inverness in two days if you want to see me again. Then I'll have to leave Scotland."

Fiona's throat burned. This was goodbye. She could see him at the Keane, a Mythean hotel and pub that protected all those within its walls from harm—even if they were criminals—but then he'd have to flee.

"I'll be there." The words felt like rocks in her throat.

He kissed her hard, then turned and pulled on the sweater.

After kissing Fluffy Black on the head to say goodbye, she followed Ian out the door of her house. She assumed she was coming back, but going up against gods would be insanely dangerous. If Carthe had more on his side...

Well, she was glad she'd said goodbye to Fluffy. Lea would take care of her if Fiona didn't return. She'd beg her to.

They walked in silence to the Praesidium. There was no need to take the car, and the fresh air grounded her in reality. They could do this. They *had* to do this.

Ian reached for Fiona's hand. Things would change after tonight. No question. If they retrieved the book, he'd either be back in prison or out of Scotland. The idea made his skin tighten and his skull squeeze his brain.

He could leave. Just walk off now and be assured of his release. Without that damn collar, one flick of his Sylph side and he'd be invisible and gone.

She'd proved she trusted him by taking off the collar. That trust... did something to him. Made him want to stay to help her. No one except Logan had ever trusted him before. It made him want to stay to help.

He'd leave after. He'd have to.

Too soon, they stood at the door of Lea's office. Lea, Aerten, Vivenne, and two Mythean Guardians were waiting for them when they walked into the expansive library.

He nodded at Lea and Aerten.

"Ready?" Aerten asked.

"Aye," Ian said in tandem with Fiona.

Aerten's eyes flicked to his high-necked sweater and lingered for the briefest second. Her brow creased.

Did she know that there was no collar beneath?

Aerten turned and indicated the warriors next to her. Ian frowned. If Aerten did know, it seemed that she didn't care.

"This is Loras." Aerten gestured to the woman.

Loras nodded at them. She was tall and slender, with daggers strapped to her thighs and a sword to her back. Her iron-gray eyes betrayed her species. She was a Ferro, one with iron strength. Despite her size, she was likely stronger than the hulking male guardian next to her.

"And this is Karrem. He's a guardian as well, but also on the university council." Aerten's voice had a hint of subtext to it that let Ian know that this was the bloke who would insure that he was taken back to prison when this is all over.

Karrem nodded at them, a big male with a hard face and weapons strapped to almost every inch of his body.

"They'll go with you and provide backup," Aerten said.

"All right," Fiona said. "Are we ready to go?"

Vivienne nodded. "I'll take the guardians first. Then I'll come back for you."

The guardians joined her and she took their hands. She closed her eyes and said, "Here goes nothing."

They disappeared.

Fiona's hand grabbed his, her palm warm and strong as she squeezed. He closed his eyes.

It was goodbye. Had to be.

As soon as they got to Dalen, the end was near. He'd need to be out of here as soon as it was over, on his way to the continent or America if he could escape.

He squeezed back, his heart feeling too tight in his chest.

Vivienne reappeared moments later. She gestured to them. "Hurry."

A second after she grabbed their hands, he felt the floor fall away. When his vision cleared, they stood in an empty alley in an ancient city. The stone was all bleached white, the ground the same. Silence prevailed.

Loras and Karrem waited, their weapons drawn. Loras' eyes roved the street at the end of the alley. Karrem's eyes were on him.

"I feel it," Fiona said.

He nodded. The book tugged at him too, as it had in the vault. It was farther away, but obvious all the same.

"This way." He set off down they alley, Fiona at his side and the guardians at front and back. Vivienne stuck close to Loras.

They hesitated at the entrance to the street. Two-story buildings lined the street, their white stone facades watching silently. It hadn't been evident in the alley, but up close, the buildings were falling apart, stones missing and entire walls downed. They saw no one, and the city streets possessed a distinct air of abandonment.

"No people," Fiona whispered. "And no guards."

"The war," Loras said. "And they don't expect invaders."

Of course. These gods had fought so viciously and so thoroughly that they'd alienated many of their believers. As a result, the afterworld must have decayed.

No wonder Carthe was hoping to destroy the covenant and find new followers. He hoped to revitalize his afterworld with the power of mortal belief. At least, it was the only explanation Ian could think of.

"To the left," Fiona said. "In the direction of the building on the hill."

They set off toward the hill at the edge of town, upon which sat a white stone monstrosity in better condition than the rest of the buildings. There wasn't much cover, but they did their best to stay in the shadows of the buildings.

Halfway to their destination, they passed several souls wandering a side street. They were dressed in ancient clothing, robes that fell around their shoulders and laced leather boots. The souls turned to stare, but unlike the gods, weren't concerned with defending the afterworld.

When they reached the edge of town, Ian halted with the rest. A field of grass separated the edge of town from the hill. Up close, it looked more like a manmade mound upon which the city's finest building had been constructed. A long flight of white stone steps climbed the side of the mound to the portico and great double doors.

"We should skirt around the edge," Ian said.

"Aye."

"Agreed."

They raced across the field, heading left when they reached the bottom of the mound and circling the base. There were no stairs at the back, nor had there been any on the side of the mound.

Silently, they climbed to the top and pressed themselves against the edge of the building between the windows. The structure was built in a style Ian was certain hadn't been common thousands of years ago, but then, gods weren't bound by technology as mortals were.

"We'll go through the window," Karrem said.

Fiona looked over. "But the noise."

"Not a problem." Karrem touched the glass, and it dissolved.

Ian's brows rose. So Karrem had hidden talents.

One by one, they climbed through the window into a wide hallway. It was flagged with white stone and had barren walls. Everything in this afterworld was white and barren, Ian realized. Whether it was natural or a product of neglect, he couldn't tell.

"To the left," Fiona whispered

Ian followed, fighting the pull of dozens of other precious artifacts, focusing instead on the call of the book that Fiona also felt.

When he heard voices, he pulled up short, breath held. The others followed suit.

"Destroy it now!" a harsh voice echoed through the hall.

"We wait for Celiae!"

They hadn't destroyed it yet? Ian's muscles would have sagged in relief had he not been so tense. They listened for a minute longer. Ian desperately tried to pick out voices.

Fiona held up her hand, three fingers raised. He agreed. From what he could hear, there were only three gods within.

But they were *gods*. More powerful than any of their party by far.

"Ready?" Loras mouthed.

He nodded, his eyes on Fiona, then became invisible. He crept toward the open door on silent feet. If he could just get in and snatch the book, the others wouldn't have to act as backup. Fiona would be safe.

Their odds against three gods were terrible, especially since Vivienne would have to stay out of the way so as not to be killed. She was their only way out.

He braced himself and stepped into the room.

CHAPTER FOURTEEN

Fiona's heart thundered as she watched Ian disappear. She squinted, hoping to see him go into the room, then realized how stupid she was being. He was invisible.

But she was so damn scared for him. The seconds ticked by like hours. Her palm sweated around her sword hilt and she shifted her feet.

A shout sounded from within. She sprang into action, sprinting for the door, the others on her heels.

She skidded into the room, taking in the scene in a glance. Three gods grappled with the air, no doubt grabbing an invisible Ian. All three of them were on him. There was no way he could hold onto the book.

She sprinted toward the closest one, a slender, black-robed figure near the back of the room. She plunged her sword into his back.

He stumbled away, releasing an invisible Ian. Karrem and Loras attacked the other two, slashing their weapons at the gods, who turned to fight back.

The god she'd stabbed turned to her. Tattoos covered his face and hands, black ink and white skin making the acid-green eyes glow. The book was clutched in his hand.

She thrust her sword again, this time into his chest. His mouth gaped, fury and shock lighting his eyes.

"Who are you?" The words gurgled from his sagging mouth. He raised his hand. A ball of glowing light formed in his palm, something hotter than fire. The heat of it blasted her skin, though it was nowhere near her.

Oh shite. Fiona jerked her sword free and swung at the god's arm. Too late. The ball of plasma flew free, aimed straight at her.

Pain. A huge force knocked her to the side. She crashed to the marble floor, falling as the god did, her eyes locked on his face. He crashed to the ground, his eyes closed and a gaping wound in his chest from her sword.

Fiona scrambled to her feet and spun around, terrified that she was correct about what had knocked her aside.

Ian lay sprawled on the marble, his sword on the ground a few feet from him, his invisibility fallen away. His handsome face was pale, his eyes closed. She raced to his side, dropped to her knees next to him.

"Ian!" She shook him.

His eyes popped open and he shook his head as if to clear it.

"I'm fine." His voice was rough, pain in every syllable.

She patted her hands over him, feeling for injuries as she glanced over her shoulder at the fray behind her. Loras and Karrem fought two gods, while the one she'd felled was prone on the ground. Vivienne was hurtling toward them.

Fiona turned back to Ian. At his side she found a great hole in his sweater and a segment of burned flesh. It was blackened and raw looking.

It could have killed him. She shook the fear away and scrambled toward the fallen god. She grabbed at the book still clutched in his hand. His grasp tightened and his eyes blazed. He was healing from his wounds and would be on his feet any second.

She plunged her sword through his neck. She left the blade protruding from his flesh and grabbed the book, then scrambled back to Ian's side.

Vivienne fell to her knees next to them and reached for their hands. "Come on!"

She gasped, then reached for Vivienne's hand. Within a second, they were back in Lea's office. The colorful book-lined shelves were such a contrast to Dalen's paleness.

Vivienne returned to the fray immediately, leaving them in the silent office. No doubt Lea was far back in the cavernous, library-like space.

Fiona cupped Ian's face in her hands. Gods, he was so beautiful to her. So reckless. She kissed him hard, then pushed him away. She knew she was risking everything with her career if she lost him. But she didn't care. She couldn't bear the thought of him being sent back to that stone box.

"Go! Use your invisibility." Her voice rushed out of her, desperate.

He staggered slightly, his face pale from the pain. He flickered in and out of sight, too weak to fully utilize his power.

"Run." Her heart felt like it was trying to tear itself away from her body.

"I'll see you," he said, his eyes dark and deep, then he turned. He was through the door and out of her sight before the sob broke from her chest.

Vivienne appeared with Karrem and Loras.

"Where is he?" Loras demanded.

"Long gone," Fiona lied. Oh gods, she had to buy him some time.

Karrem charged out of the room, Loras on his heels.

Nay! Fiona ran after them, rounding the corner in time to see a dagger strike Ian in the back. He was nearly to the end of the hallway, but Karrem was too fast. He threw another dagger and Ian stumbled. Fell to his knees.

"Nay!" she screamed.

But it did no good. Loras and Karrem were upon him, grabbing his arms and hauling him to his feet. Blood dripped to the floor.

Fiona watched, helpless, as they dragged Ian down the hall.

CHAPTER FIFTEEN

Three weeks later
Prison for Magical Deviants, Immortal University
Edinburgh, Scotland

Rough hands shoved Ian into his cell. The heavy metal door slammed shut behind him, the footsteps of the prison guard echoing down the hallway. Ian dragged a hand down his face, sighing disgustedly at the feel of the grit on his skin. The prison guards had just escorted him back from construction duty in Moloch.

Building the cathedral in hell had been worse than ever since he'd been thrown back in here three weeks ago. His brief taste of freedom—and having Fiona—had only served to highlight the misery of the prison.

There'd been no retrial when he'd been captured after the assault on Dalen. They'd simply pulled the daggers from his back, patched him up, and thrown him back in the cell. He'd managed to slip the collar back around his neck in the infirmary. To his knowledge, no one had noticed that it had ever been gone, so Fiona shouldn't take the blame.

It was the least he could do for her. She'd tried to free him.

If she'd tried to visit him while he was down here, he had no idea. Hell, visits probably weren't even allowed.

He sat on his bed and pulled the dirty boots from his feet. Another endless day of mortaring stone and then breaking it down again. Compared to the exhilaration of being with Fiona, it was an exercise in utter misery.

The lock on his cell door creaked. His head jerked up. No one should be turning that lock until tomorrow morning, when he'd head back to Moloch.

An unfamiliar guard walked in and shut the door behind him.

"Who the hell are you?" he asked. But even as he said it, his skin prickled.

It couldn't be.

Green magic swirled around the figure. When it dissipated, Logan stood inside his cell.

Hope flared in Ian's chest. "How the hell are you here? Warding spells bar you from the campus." As a god, Logan wasn't allowed on the campus of the Immortal University. In an attempt to maintain peace between the afterworlds, the university sometimes made decisions that the gods didn't like. Hence the need for the spell that banned them from the grounds unless they were granted permission to be there.

Logan grinned. "Not pleased to see me?"

"Aye." Ian strode to his friend and hugged him, clapping him on the back. "But how the hell did you waltz right in here? You aren't allowed on the grounds."

"I have a little trick up my sleeve."

"Trick? Why the hell did you no' use that trick a hundred years ago to get me out of here? I took the fall for us back then."

Guilt flashed in Loki's dark eyes. "I didn't have it then. In fact, I only recently obtained it."

Ian frowned. "The trade with the god? That was about getting me out of prison? I thought you planned for me to escape after I retrieved the book."

"You're right. I hadn't intended to come here." Loki looked around the small stone cell, his brow furrowed with distaste. "I wanted the charm that gets me past the university enchantments for other reasons. But my damn conscience kept tugging at me."

"You do have one, you know, no matter how much you might protest." And Logan always did protest. True, he did whatever the hell he wanted and his own endgame was always of the utmost importance, but whenever he'd been given an opportunity to do right, Ian had watched him take it.

"Thinking of you still in here, after all these years." Logan shook his head, regret plain on his face. "You saved my life when we first met, and again when you took the blame for what happened at the museum. And you've kept my identity a secret. I should have tried harder to do something sooner. To get you out of here. We were partners."

"Aye, we were." They had been good times.

"I've been keeping an eye on Fiona."

Ian's heart thudded.

"She's miserable," Loki said. "Tries to visit you, weeps all the time in her cottage. She recently left Scotland, headed I don't know where."

Misery surged through Ian's veins. "Then let's get out of here."

"We can't."

"Shite. 'Course not." The cell had magic in place that would alert the guards if it were ever empty when it wasn't supposed to be. "Why the hell did you join me here if you canna get us out?"

Green mist swirled around Logan until Ian was looking at a mirror image of himself. Same face, same build, same clothes covered in the dirt of hell.

"Because it's my turn."

CHAPTER SIXTEEN

Three days later
Off the coast of Spain

Fiona stared morosely at the horizon. Blazing sun beat down on the little boat, a rusted barge that had seen better days and now floated tranquilly on the deep blue Mediterranean. Spain could be seen a couple miles away, flat and baking in the sun.

The tropical heat should have made her feel better. It didn't.

"Are you okay?" Claire asked.

Fiona turned to look at her colleague. She'd been paired with Claire on this project a week ago. Their job was to find an ancient Greek artifact on the shipwreck below and return it to the university for conservation. They were based in a little town called Murcia that was so full of pink British tourists that Fiona felt like she'd never left Scotland. Even the nice weather and nicer food couldn't keep her mind off home.

"Fine," Fiona said, trying to distract herself from her misery. The fact that she didn't have the clearance to visit Ian made it even worse. No one could visit prisoners in that ward. She'd tried every day to visit him and been stopped at the desk. It had driven her crazy with misery until she could barely get off her couch.

When the university had wanted to send her on this project with Claire, she'd jumped at the chance to get into a new environment, hoping that it would break the cycle of ice cream eating while sniffling—she was a total cliché—and weeping into Fluffy Black's fur.

Her heart had stung unbearably when she'd boarded the plane for Spain, and landing in Cartagena hadn't made her feel any better. At least Fluffy Black could come with her. Years ago, after a terrible illness, Fluffy had been bespelled to be immortal. Like a witch's familiar, but without the magic. She was connected to Fiona in a way that allowed her to follow Fiona on her trips, move from place to place, and not get put out like a normal cat.

She helped Fiona cope, even when she felt like an idiot for mourning a man she'd known for so short a time. And Claire had been really nice, she realized absently. She'd kept Fiona company while she'd drowned her sorrows in pints of Estrella and plates of tapas in the evening. The chill water always snapped her into work mode the next day, and it became easy to help Claire find the historic treasures she sought for the university collections.

The artifact at their feet was their biggest find of all, easily located at the edge of a small ballast pile and under some sand. Without her bloodhound senses for artifacts, it would have taken mortal archaeologists months or years to properly excavate and find the thing. For Fiona, it was the work of a dive, even when she was distracted by thoughts of Ian. The artifact they'd just found—another ancient computer-like device like the Greek Antikythera mechanism—should have thrilled her. It didn't. She could barely care.

"Seriously, Fiona. I haven't known you long, but I can tell you're totally bummed about something," Claire said.

Bummed was one way to put it, Fiona thought, as she looked out at the flat blue ocean. She'd been reinstated as an Acquirer for the Department of Magical Devices for two and a half weeks. Ian had been back in prison for three.

"Ready to go back to port?" the captain called from behind the wheel.

Fiona's head snapped up and she realized she'd been ignoring Claire. The sympathy in her new friend's eyes made her own sting. Relief rushed through her when Claire turned away and yelled an assent to the captain. Holding it together was always easier when people weren't being nice. It was like the dam she'd built up against her feelings got a crack in it every time someone was sympathetic to her misery.

Nothing was like she'd expected it to be when she'd dreamed of finding the book again. True, she felt the contentment she'd always expected from fulfilling her fate. She no longer had the threat of madness looming over her shoulder. She had her job back. She'd saved the world from the threat of divine war.

So everything should be perfect, she thought as she gazed out at the sun sparkling on the sea. She'd accomplished more than she'd ever hoped and had been reinstated to her old post with commendations and glory. Ian must have kept the collar and slipped it back on when Karrem and Loras had captured him. It was the only explanation for why she hadn't been fired for letting him escape. They thought he'd simply overpowered her.

Yet without Ian, the victory was hollow. She enjoyed the work, but the evenings were spent with food and her cat. Both of which were good, but didn't quite cut it.

Fed up with her own moping, Fiona pushed away from the boat's rail and went up to the bow to grab the bow line and help Claire and the captain bring the boat into the dock.

They motored past dozens of small boats that sat cheek by jowl in their slips, all rolling on the light wake of the barge, their metal dangling bits clanking musically against masts and hulls.

It really was beautiful, she thought. Fat lot of good it did her. The captain pulled the boat into the slip and she and Claire tied off.

"I'll take care of the dive kit," she said.

"Are you sure?" Claire asked.

"No problem. I know you've got a date." Claire had been over the moon about the fact that her boyfriend was visiting from Scotland.

"Thanks! I'll make it up to you!" Claire grabbed her day bag and ran up the dock.

After checking the lines and the engine, the captain trundled after her, his lunch sack flopping against his thigh with every step. He'd leave her to clean up her dive gear, since his only concern was the boat.

Fiona sighed and turned back to the boat. She was hauling the air tanks off the deck when she caught sight of a tall figure striding down the dock, passing behind the occasional mast or pilothouse, which cut him off from her view.

They'd been coming out here every day for a week and had yet to see the weekenders on their boats. It was Friday and only about two in the afternoon, so maybe he was getting the day started early. Just another boater.

But she squinted harder, unsure of why he caught her eye. She could barely make out his face or his—

Her heart dropped her feet.

Ian.

It was Ian striding down the dock, his steps long and sure on the bobbing surface. But how? He should be locked up a thousand miles away back in Edinburgh.

She stared dumbly. Ian was only five meters away now, so close she could see the green of his eyes. A smile kicked up the corner of his mouth and still she stared, blindsided and stupid.

Soon, Ian was standing in front of her, something she'd dreamed about in her wildest imagination yet never expected in a thousand years.

"Hello." He held out a hand for the heavy tank in her arms.

"Hi." She dumbly handed it to him.

He set it down on its side.

"Oh my gods, you're here!" It finally hit her and she leapt off the boat, stumbling onto the dock like a moron but past caring.

She threw her arms around him, laughing when he swept her up and squeezed her to him.

"How?" she asked against his shoulder. "How are you here?"

"Long story."

"Gods, you have to tell me all of it. I just canna believe it. Are you out? For good?" She leaned back and looked at his face, thinner than when she'd last seen it, but so handsome her heart felt like it would burst.

"I am."

"Good." She kissed him, hard and fast, joy in every movement.

"Gods, I've missed you," Ian muttered against Fiona's lips.

"Likewise." She pulled him onto the boat and into the pilothouse. Thank gods the captain had left. "I want to hear about how you got out, but no' yet."

She tore at his shirt, pulling it over his head and throwing it to the floor. She wrapped her arms around his neck and pressed her mouth to his, hot and warm and so perfect.

Within seconds, he had her pants around her ankles and she kicked them off. She reached out greedily for his cock, and a fierce wave of satisfaction roared through him when he felt her hand.

"Wait." His voice was rough as he reached between her legs. "I need to make sure you're ready for me."

An animal noise escaped her when his fingers parted her sex, slipping between the slick folds to stroke. Soon she was wet and trembling, her need and joy clear.

"Now," she gasped.

"Aye." He picked her up and pressed her against the wall of the pilothouse, then brought her down upon his cock. He thrust inside of her, groaning at the feeling of her wet heat enveloping him.

She arched against him, picking up a rhythm that matched his own.

Soon they were straining against one another, desperate to chase away the memory of their separation. She was lean and strong, her body an intoxicant.

Gods, he was going to come too soon.

He grabbed the rail on the ceiling, focusing on the bite of the wood into his palm instead of on the wet heat of her pussy. It didn't work.

Ah, gods, he was going to lose it. With a groan, he pulled free and slid down her body. He propped her against the wall and set his mouth to her. Her cry of frustration was replaced with one of pleasure.

She was gloriously wet and slick, and when he thrust his tongue inside of her, he tasted the bite of his own pre-cum. A beastly possessiveness in him made him growl against her, the animal he'd professed to have contained.

Desperate to get her off before he lost it all over the floor, he moved his mouth to her clitoris and pushed two fingers inside of her. The feel of her heat closing over him drew a groan from him and he stroked her with his tongue.

Within seconds, her whole body stiffened and her hips pushed against his face, her pussy spasming around his fingers.

Fuck.

He withdrew from her and rose up quickly, thrusting inside of her so that he could feel the remnants of her orgasm. She cried out and clutched his shoulders as he lifted her, her face flushed and beautiful.

His hips lost any semblance of rhythm or grace as a second orgasm tore through her and lit up his own. He heaved over her, lost. A guttural cry escaped his lips as his back arched and the orgasm pounded up through his shaft and broke him apart.

When it was done, he saw nothing but white light and collapsed against her, held up by sheer luck. Dimly, he recognized that she was still shuddering from her orgasm, perhaps in the grips of another. But as much as he wanted to reach a hand down to her clitoris to help her along, he hadn't an ounce of strength in his body.

A minute later, once she'd stilled and he'd caught at least a bit of his breath, he opened his eyes to see her looking at him, a satisfied smile on her face.

"Apparently we just had to get that out of our system," she said.

He laughed roughly and scrubbed a hand over his face. "I guess I was worried I'd never get to again."

She grinned, an energy and a lightness about her that he'd never seen while they were on the hunt for the book. "And these are some big windows in this pilothouse. Thank gods the marina is empty. Now tell me how you got out."

He looked over at her, memorizing the face that was so new to him, yet so cherished.

A cloud drifted over the perfection of the afternoon. "Logan got me out."

Her head whipped toward him. "Really?"

"Aye. We've been friends for ages—you were right about that. He was my partner when I robbed the Scottish Museum of Antiquities and was there the night it blew up. He was never caught for it." He thought back to what Logan had told him. "It bothered him that I took the fall, especially since I saved his life when we first met. And I've kept his secret."

"Secret?"

"Aye." Logan had given him permission to tell her. "Logan is actually the god Loki."

"Are you serious? He's been missing for centuries!"

"Not missing, just hiding. He can shapeshift, which helps."

"And he took your place?" Disbelief tinged her voice.

"Logan does no' care for many, but when he does, it's true. It was his turn, he said."

"Wow. Just, wow. I never would have expected that. He's so damn ruthless and self-interested, at least according to the myths."

"It's who the mortals created him to be. They believed him to be that, so he was. But ideas have a life of their own. Loki's his own man. Though they've been created by belief, all the gods are. They're no' always what we think they are."

"Nay, I suppose no'. But how'd he get you out?"

"He figured out a way to get on campus and took my place in the cell." Guilt ate at him, a gnawing sensation that chewed at his insides. But he'd get Logan out.

"How is that even possible?"

"He got onto the campus using whatever Carthe gave him in exchange for the Book of Worlds." Though from what Loki had said in the cell, he hadn't been intending to use it to free Ian. He wanted to be on campus for another reason, though Ian didn't know what it was. "He used his shapeshifting ability to sneak in under the guise of one of the guards."

"And you used your invisibility to get out?"

"Aye. I walked out of the prison behind another when he opened the main door."

"Oh my gods. So you're on the run from the university?"

Dread sent a spike through Ian's gut. "Aye. Logan is in my prison cell, shapeshifted into my form. I canna go back to Scotland or they'll know something is amiss." And he couldn't go back until he had a way to free Loki.

"Oh, shite."

The distress in her tone twisted his heart. This was what he'd been afraid of. She wanted to work for the university. He couldn't go anywhere near the place.

"I know it's been such a short period of time," he said. "And I'm no' expecting you to profess love or want to marry me right out of the gate, but I want to keep seeing you. I care for you, Fiona. More than I've ever cared for anyone."

She kissed him. "I wanted to visit you, but could no'. I dinna have clearance for some reason. I came to Spain to try to get over some of the pain of losing you, but it's no' working. I doona even enjoy working for the university anymore."

"I'm sorry. You wanted it so badly."

"I thought I did. But I want to be with you. I'll go with you. We'll hunt for artifacts on our own."

He grinned, joy singing through him.

"But no' for money. We canna sell them. We have to turn them over to a museum for conservation and display. I doona know how we'll fund it, but we'll find a way. Could you be happy like that?"

"As long as you and I are creeping around old tombs and archaeological sites finding treasure, I'll be just fine. And I can fund the expeditions. The money I put in the bank before I was imprisoned has done quite well. Interest is an amazing thing."

Her jaw slackened. "Interest? Over a hundred years? That's enormous."

"Aye. And I know just what we'll go hunting for first."

"What?"

He dug into his pocket and pulled out a folded piece of paper. "Logan gave me this when he got me out. Whatever is at the end of this map will get Loki out of prison. After that, it's just you, me, and adventure."

"And Fluffy Black."

He smiled. "Aye."

She leaned up and kissed him. "I think I love you."

A warmth burst in his chest that pushed out any coldness. He pulled her down to him for a hard kiss. "I think it's more than mutual."

She grinned, and in her smile he saw the light of a future brighter than any he'd ever imagined.

THANK YOU!

Thank you so much for reading *Stolen Fate*. I loved writing this story and hope you enjoyed reading it!

If you'd like to know when my next book is available, you can join my new release newsletter at http://linseyhall.com/

Reviews help other readers discover books and are vitally important to authors. I appreciate all reviews, both positive and negative, and I really appreciate the time you take if you choose to leave one. Click here to do so.

I love to hear from readers. Connect with me on twitter at @HiLinseyHall. Or find me on Facebook at https://www.facebook.com/LinseyHallAuthor

If you liked *Stolen Fate*, the other books in the series are *Braving Fate*, *Soulceress*, and *Rogue Soul,* and they're available now.

AUTHOR'S NOTE

The museum in this book, called the Scottish Museum of Antiquities, was based off of the real National Museum of Scotland, located in Edinburgh. The National Museum is an amazing place, full of artifacts and history from dozens of periods.

The cat in this story, Fluffy Black, is based off of a very sweet stray cat who came into our lives for too short a period. Illness took her too soon, so I tried to immortalize her here, in the pages of *Stolen Fate*. I hope you liked her, and will consider adopting a stray cat or dog if they ever come into your life (perhaps you already have :-).

GLOSSARY

Aether - The invisible substance that connects the afterworlds and earth. It is both nothing and everything.

Aetherwalking - A method of traveling through the aether to access the afterworlds or different places on earth. Some Mytheans have this power and can bring another person with them.

Afterworld - A heaven or hell created by mortal belief. Mortals can access them only through death. Some Mytheans can aetherwalk to them.

Immortal University - An organization created thousands of years ago to protect Mytheans and keep them secret from mortals. It was initially founded as a true university, hence the name, but over time it morphed into an institution with greater power and responsibility. The university's primary goal is to maintain the secrecy of Mytheans and to keep the gods from warring to obtain more followers. They do this primarily through diplomacy. The university also provides services to Mytheans that they can't get elsewhere, lest mortals figure out that their clients never die. Things like education, health services, and banking.

Historious - Mytheans who have the ability to locate valuable artwork and artifacts, as well as perform a limited amount of magic. Their long-dead ancestors had been disciples of the Celtic god Gwydion, a god of magic and the arts. The skill had passed down through the generations, which were few, as immortals rarely reproduced.

Mortals - Humans. They are unaware of the existence of Mytheans or that all heavens and hells truly exist. They are immortal in the sense that their soul will pass on to whatever afterworld they believe in.

Mythean - Supernatural individuals created by mortal belief. They are gods and goddesses, demons and monsters, witches and other supernatural creatures. They are immortal in the sense that if they live on earth, only beheading or grievous injury from magic can kill them. If they are killed their soul will pass on to an afterworld. Secrecy from mortals is one of their highest priorities. Some Mytheans, particularly species of demons and some gods, are trapped in their afterworlds. Others have access to both earth and the afterworlds.

Mythean Guardians - Powerful mortals made immortal, or other supernatural beings who serve at the Praesidium. They protect those mortals and Mytheans who are important to the fate of humanity.

Praesidium - The protection division of the Immortal University. Mythean Guardians work here. Their job is to protect those important to humanity and maintain law and order by keeping Mytheans secret from humans and keeping the gods from warring.

Soulceresses - Mytheans who fuel their power by draining the immortal power of other Mytheans' souls. When fueled by the power of others, they can manifest their magic with a thought. They are hated by other Mytheans because of this. They also have the ability to see the evil in a person's soul.

Sylph - An ancient air spirit from a religion that is lost to memory. Sylphs and their descendents have the ability to attain invisibility by becoming one with the air. They are also able to manipulate the wind.

Books by Linsey Hall

Braving Fate
Soulceress
Rogue Soul
Stolen Fate

ABOUT LINSEY

Before becoming a romance novelist, Linsey Hall was a nautical archaeologist who studied shipwrecks from Hawaii and the Yukon to the UK and the Mediterranean. She credits the historical romances of the 70's, 80's, and 90's with her love of history and her career as an archaeologist. After a decade of tromping around the globe in search of old bits of stuff that people left lying about, she settled down and started penning her own romance novels. Her debut series, the Mythean Arcana, draws upon her love of history and the paranormal elements that she can't help but include. Several books may or may not feature her cats.

This is a work of fiction. All reference to events, persons, and locale are used fictitiously, except where documented in historical record. Names, characters, and places are products of the author's imagination, and any resemblance to actual events, locales, or persons, living or dead, is coincidental.

Copyright 2014 by Linsey Hall
Published by Bonnie Doon Press LLC
Paperback Edition 1.0

All rights reserved, including the right of reproduction in whole or in part in any form, except in instances of quotation used in critical articles or book review. Where such permission is sufficient, the author grants the right to strip any DRM which may be applied to this work.

Linsey@LinseyHall.com
www.LinseyHall.com
https://twitter.com/HiLinseyHall
https://www.facebook.com/LinseyHallAuthor

BONNIE
DOON
PRESS

ISBN 978-1-942085-30-0 (eBook)
ISBN 978-1-942085-31-7 (Paperback)

www.ingramcontent.com/pod-product-compliance
Lightning Source LLC
Chambersburg PA
CBHW020256130626
46549CB00005B/2243